SECRET IDENTITY

THE SECRET SERIES

JILL SANDERS

GRAYTON

To my family,
whom I could never forget.

SUMMARY

Eve is at the top of her game. She's finally going to make partner at the ad agency run by two of her best friends. But when she takes a business trip to wine and dine a potential customer, her boss decides to tag along at the last minute. Now everything she's worked hard for might just disappear in a flash.

Carter has had a thing for his best friend Eve ever since he can remember. He hired her a few years ago to help boost his business and it has never run more smoothly. But when a once-in-a-lifetime opportunity presents itself, he takes a chance at happiness that could end up destroying their friendship.

Carter watched Eve from across the room. For the last ten years of his life, he'd watched her every chance he could. He would consider himself a borderline stalker if she wasn't one of his best friends. He didn't know if she knew that he watched her or if she knew how he felt, but he wasn't ready to risk it. Yet.

A few hours later, however, he'd had the right mix of lack of food, too much sun, and too much beer. When he'd walked into his grandparents' old place, he'd accidentally bumped into her in the upstairs hallway. He hadn't even known she was in the house. He'd thought she was still outside with the many other guests, either on the dock soaking up the sun, or out on the boat, water skiing. But there she was, just outside his grandparents' old bedroom. Instincts had kicked in and before he knew it, he'd pushed her through the door, shutting it with his foot as he'd swooped in for the most fantastic kiss he'd ever had. She'd tasted like strawberries and felt smoother than silk as he'd run his hands over her half-naked body. For a split second, he thought she'd arched into him and relaxed into the kiss. But then they had heard a cough and a click, then jumped apart like they'd been caught kissing, and well, they had. By one of Eve's best friends, Susan.

For the next week, Carter hadn't known how to approach her. Or what to say. Did he say anything? Or act like nothing had happened.

When he had finally approached her, she'd looked at her feet and told him she was getting married to her long-time boyfriend, Steve. His heart had been broken. That night he'd gone out with Mitch, his other best friend, and over their second pitcher of beer, they'd come up with a business plan that had rocketed them to the big times.

The next years of his life were a blur. He and Mitch spent all their time building their ad agency, Kovich & Edwards Agency, into a multimillion-dollar business. He'd stayed focused and every time he'd seen Eve, he'd tried not to think about that perfect kiss one hot summer day in Maine.

But when Carter had walked into his office a few years later to see Eve crying and sitting next to Mitch, he'd realized he had one more chance at happiness.

"I caught Steve cheating on me," she blurted out and he could see she was on the verge of tears.

"Carter, I've just saved our butts. I hired Eve to take over the Johnson contract. Actually, she's going to be taking half your clients, so you can have some more time in the office to straighten out the mess." Mitch smiled at Eve and patted her hand as she sniffled into a Kleenex.

"What?" Carter just stood there, and if his mind hadn't been so focused on how beautiful Eve was, even red-eyed, he probably could have pieced together what his friend was saying.

"You don't have to hire me," Eve said as she wiped her eyes.

Carter's mind jumped into gear. Eve was single. For the first time in almost eight years, she was single again. There was no way he was going to let this opportunity slip by him again.

He slowly walked over and sat across from her, really taking in how she looked. He could no longer see her red swollen eyes, but only how she'd looked that day in his grandparents' bedroom: wet, half-naked, and in his arms. Not to mention the feel of her skin under his hands or the taste of her lips. "No, it's fine. Welcome aboard." He smiled and knew it was going to be the hardest thing in the world working with the woman he desired so much.

CHAPTER 1

She could hear talking, but every time she tried to focus, she would slip back into the darkness. One voice stood out, however; it was constantly there. Its richness warmed her. She felt hands on her, cold hands. They came and went, lifting her, moving her, but she didn't respond. It was almost as if her mind was locked in a room, unable to respond to anything.

Finally, it was quiet, and she slept. Then there was a bright light and she squinted as she raised her arms up to shield her eyes from the light.

"Eve?" The deep voice said just above her.

"Eve?" She opened her eyes and saw a dark-haired man leaning over her. She blinked a few times, trying to get his face into better focus. Her eyes refused to focus at first; she looked up at him as if seeing him through a haze. Finally, he came into focus and she noticed his chocolate eyes hovered just above hers. There was a thick covering of stubble on his chin, and it was obvious that he hadn't shaved in a while. She ran her eyes slowly over the nice shape of his jaw and wondered how it would feel if she reached up and ran her fingers over it. His hair was messed up, like he'd run his hands through it. Would it be as soft as it looked? His shirt buttons were open, and she saw dried blood spots around the neck.

She went to move, to try and wipe her eyes. "No, sweetie," he said in the rich voice she'd come to know. "Don't move. Your wrist is sprained." He held her other hand and for the first time, she noticed a dull pain radiating from her left wrist.

Someone else spoke from across the room. He looked up, away from her, to answer them. When he looked back down at her, he smiled. "Mitchell and Sandi are here. Sandi's going to go find a doctor." She watched a tear slip down his cheek. Raising her good hand, she wiped it from his face. The wetness on her fingertips felt warm.

"Hey there." Another head leaned over her. This one was blond, and the man had sea green eyes. He too looked like he could use a shave. The worry in both their eyes matched.

"I…" Her throat felt sore. She cleared it and tried to talk again, but just as she opened her mouth this time, the doctor walked in.

"Hi, good morning. I hear our patient is up."

"Yes," the men said in unison.

"Good." An older, gray-haired man leaned over her now. His face was wrinkled, and he had kind, blue eyes. "How are you feeling? Mrs. Taylor?"

She blinked a few times and fear crept into her mind. "I…Where am I?" She didn't know what to say. She had so many questions, but this one seemed to be the most important at the moment.

"You're at University Hospital in Chicago." Then the older man looked up, away from her. "If you don't mind, I'd like to examine her. Maybe you can run downstairs for a cup of coffee?" She heard people leaving the room and the click of the door being shut.

A young, blonde nurse leaned over her now. "Here, would you like to sit up?" The bed began moving and soon she was looking at a small, empty hospital room. She could see her feet tucked under a large green blanket. She wiggled her toes and saw the blanket move.

"Good. I see you moving your feet." The nurse smiled at her.

"Can you tell me, what's the last thing you remember?" The doctor flashed a light at her face and her head exploded. She shut her eyes and grabbed her head with her good hand. Pain spread from her left temple down her jaw, through her neck, and into her entire body.

"I'm sorry, dear. I know your eyes are sensitive to the light, but I have to check your pupils. Can you open your eyes for me?"

She shook her head slightly. The pain was almost too much to bear.

"Okay, we can try again later. Can you tell me how many fingers I'm holding up?" She slowly opened her eyes and looked. It was blurry, but she could see three fingers.

"Three."

"Good. How's your vision? Can you see the clock on the wall there?" He pointed across the room. She could just make out a dark circle but wouldn't have known it was a clock. She shook her head.

"Okay, that's okay. Sometimes a bump on the head like the one you took will play havoc with your sight. It may take a few days until everything is back in focus." She watched him write something down. "Can you tell me the last thing you remember?"

She thought about it. The last thing she remembered. Everything was blurry. She was in a hospital room in Chicago. There was a dark-haired man whose voice was familiar to her, a blond man named Mitchell, and someone named Sandi. Looking up at the doctor, she shook her head, no.

"No? No, you can't tell me what happened? Or no, you don't remember what happened to you?"

"I don't remember anything." She felt the bedspread under her fingers and gripped the cotton. She felt short of breath and found it difficult to swallow. "I can't remember anything. Who I am. Who those people were. Why I'm in Chicago. I can't even remember what I look like or my name."

Two days earlier

Eve couldn't believe her eyes. For the millionth time in her life, Carter Edwards was on her nerves. She watched him sprint towards her with a small black bag in hand, his usual smile pasted on his face. Most women would swoon over his dashing personality and rugged good looks. She, however, found it hard not to grind her teeth in frustration.

"Good," he said as he stopped right in front of her. "I made it." He stowed his bag in the overhead compartment and sat next to her in the aisle seat. Instantly the large plane felt smaller.

"What are you doing here?" She tried not to talk

between clenched teeth. Relaxing her jaw, she took a deep breath as she waited for him to answer her.

"There, all ready." He nodded to the flight attendant who blushed a little and turned to start her pre-flight tasks. "I decided to join you in Chicago. Tom Russell can be quite overbearing. I thought I'd tag along to help out."

He leaned back in his seat and crossed his long legs, looking rather comfortable in such a small space. She knew exactly how to handle Tom Russell—the same way she handled all her other clients and, on occasion, her boss. She squinted at him and wished he would just go away.

"How did you get the seat next to mine? This flight was booked." She looked around.

He smiled and looked at her. "I have my ways. Aww, now, don't give me that look. You won't even know I'm here."

How could she not know he was there? He seemed to suck up all the air in the compartment and she swore the walls of the plane had just moved in three feet.

She tried to relax, knowing it was going to be a long flight and trip. A few hours sitting next to Carter seemed like nothing compared to four days in Chicago with him. As the plane started to taxi, she tried not to think about how close his knee was to hers.

For years, she'd tried not to think about Carter in that way. Even when she'd been engaged to that lying, cheating...No—she interrupted her thoughts. Negative thoughts produced negative actions. She started doing her breathing exercises.

"Thinking about the scum ball again?" She heard the humor in Carter's voice and tried not to lash out at him.

"It's really none of your concern." She leaned her head back and closed her eyes.

"It is when it gets in the way of you doing your job." She heard him chuckle.

She could feel him leaning closer to her, could feel his breath on her hair. Opening her eyes, she saw how close he was to her and wanted to lean back, but she didn't. She wasn't going to give him an inch. "In case you've missed it, we are not in the office, or sitting in front of a client. What I do, or think about, on my own personal time is my business."

"Come on, Eve, we're friends, right?" He looked at her with his dark eyes and she lost all the pent-up frustration. Why did he always seem to be able to do that?

"Yes, we're friends." She smiled slightly at him.

"Good, why don't you tell your good friend Carter what's bothering you?" He turned his shoulders a little so that his body was facing her. She had always liked his shoulders and the one time she'd actually gotten her hands on them, she hadn't wanted to let go. Her mind flashed to the party he'd thrown for their graduation at his grandparents' place in Maine. She'd been wearing her favorite black bikini, and he'd been in his red swim shorts and no shirt. He'd been wet, like he'd just come out of the water, and she'd wanted nothing more than to lick the water drops from every inch of him.

Then Susan had taken that picture of them kissing. It had taken almost three months for Eve to wrangle the negatives out of her. Her only regret was not getting it before Carter had gotten a copy. Knowing he had a copy of that photo only ate her up more. They never spoke of the kiss, or the photo. The negative and picture sat in a box in her closet. But the fact that it was there, looming between them, did something to her.

"What?" He looked at her and she watched the small crease creep between his eyebrows. He had nice eyebrows, too. Actually, he had nice everything. His dark hair was always cut short, and his skin was always dark and tan due to his Greek heritage. He was tall and lean with just the amount of muscle tone that made a girl's mouth water. His dark eyes usually told his emotions before his face did. His lips were intoxicating. Her eyes traveled over him as they sat there. Then, with a jerk, the plane started rushing towards the end of the runway and she faced forward and gripped the armrests.

"Still get nervous when you fly?" He chuckled a little.

"Shut up." She closed her eyes and ran through her prayers, ending on a Hail Mary when she felt the vessel level off in the air.

"You've gotten better." When she looked, he was smiling at her. "You used to pray the entire flight."

"Well, I've been flying a lot more lately." She leaned over and removed her tablet and pulled her seat tray down. When she pulled out the small keyboard, she heard Carter sigh.

"What?" She looked at him.

"You don't have to work all the time, you know." He was frowning at her computer.

"I know. I just had a few emails I needed to send before we land." She clicked a few buttons and waited for the screen to pop up.

"They can wait. It's not like your boss is going to fire you, you know." He smiled again and this time, she smiled back.

"I've been meaning to ask you…" She turned towards him, a new plan firmly in her mind. For the past three weeks since Mitchell had announced he was getting married, she'd been trying to convince them to bring her on as partner. She'd saved enough money in the last five years to buy into the business and wanted nothing more than to be full partner. But every time she brought it up, Mitch would tell her to talk to Carter, since he was the business head and Mitchell was just the talent scout. Or so he claimed. When she tried to talk to Carter about it, somehow, he always found a way out of the conversations.

Looking around the plane, she doubted he could fake a last-minute business meeting here. Since he was cornered, she decided it was an excellent place to ask about buying in.

"Have you thought about me buying in to K&E? Did you look over the business plan I gave you?" She waited for his answer.

"Umm," he looked around, no doubt trying to find the nearest escape.

"Here," she leaned over and pulled a black folder from her bag and handed it to him. "I brought a copy of my proposal with me."

He looked at the folder in her hands and closed his eyes, faking a snore.

"You can't get away from me this time." She laughed. "Just look over it. It's not like I'm asking much. You know very well that I deserve this chance." She tossed the folder into his lap and watched him pick it up.

"I've already looked it over." He tried to hand it back to her.

"And?" She crossed her arms over her chest.

"And it's a solid business plan." He set the folder on top of her tablet on the tray in front of her.

"That's it?" She held up the folder again. "Solid?"

"Okay, it's a very solid business plan." He smiled at her and crossed his arms, mocking her.

"Carter, just tell me if you don't want me to be partner. I won't be offended." She set the folder down.

"That's not it." He frowned at her.

"What is it, then? Is my offer too low?" She opened the folder and started looking through her proposal.

"No, if anything it's too much." He looked away.

"What is it, then?" She punched out each word between gritted teeth.

He closed his eyes and sighed. "Listen, how about we grab some dinner tonight and talk about it. I know this great pizza place downtown."

She looked at him. They'd had plenty of dinners together over the years. After all, wining and dining someone was a big part of winning a potential client over. But never had he asked her to dinner, just her, and in such a casual way.

"Why can't you just talk about it now? It's not like we're going anywhere." She motioned around the almost full plane. She was trying to keep her patience in check. He really could be annoying at times. Ever since she'd first met him in middle school, he'd always had to have his way.

Actually, it was due to their friendship and her friendship with Mitchell, that she'd chosen the career path she had. If it wasn't for them, she doubted she would be living in her large apartment overlooking Central Park. She owed the two of them more than she could repay. But that didn't stop her from wanting to become partner in their ad agency. She'd worked harder than she'd ever dreamed in the last few years, building their clientele to such a high standard and number that they'd hired on several more employees just to manage all the work.

She watched as Carter leaned his head back. "I was hoping to catch some sleep. I was working until early this morning and wanted to shut down for a while." He closed his eyes and she could see a slight smile on his lips. He was avoiding her again. The question was, was she going to allow him to manipulate her so easily.

"That's fine. But I can't do dinner tonight. I am meeting Simon Thomas for dinner." She leaned back and sighed a little, watching Carter's reaction out of the corner of her eye.

"Simon?" Carter sat up a little. "Why are you meeting Simon Thomas for dinner?" She could feel his eyes boring into the side of her face. Closing her eyes, a little, it took everything she had not to smile.

"I suppose he wants to talk to me about my proposal." She said easily.

"Proposal?" She heard the anger in his voice and laughed as she opened her eyes and looked at him.

"Really, Carter. Why is it so hard to believe that another ad agency isn't willing to snatch me up? I have a solid proposal. I've proven myself worthy of being partner. My client lists are impressive, and everyone is happy with my performance. Why are you having such a hard time bringing me in? Even Mitch was on board with my proposal." She glared at him.

He leaned back and looked at her. "Do you really have a meeting with Simon tonight?"

She nodded her head and watched his eyes heat. She knew she'd struck a chord by mentioning Carter's nemesis. But the fact was, Simon had called her up when he'd found out that she'd be in Chicago and had asked her for a meeting. She hadn't sent a proposal to him, but if Carter didn't give her an answer before they landed, she was seriously thinking about making Simon an offer.

He sat there, silently, and she could tell he was boiling hot. Maybe she had crossed the line a little. But the little cat and mouse game he'd been playing over the last few weeks was tiring. She knew it was time to change who was chasing whom.

Carter stood up and reached into the overhead bin, pulling out his bag. When he sat back down, she could tell he wasn't going to give her an answer.

"Here." He set a large envelope in front of her. "One of the reasons I wanted to do dinner tonight." He set his bag on the ground and leaned back again, closing his eyes.

When she opened the large envelope, she realized she'd misjudged him. There in front of her was all the legal paperwork for her to become full partner in Kovich & Edwards Agency. All she had to do was sign her name.

She stole a glance at Carter. He was watching her with a large smile on his face. "How about canceling that dinner with Simon Thomas and we'll celebrate with pizza and beer?"

She laughed and smiled at him. "Sounds like a plan, partner."

Carter relaxed back in his seat and tried not to show his

excitement. He'd been upset when Eve had mentioned Simon Thomas's name. The man just got under his skin. Ever since his college days, Simon had followed him around, trying to show him up. Of course, it had helped that Carter had his best friends there, where Simon had always been a loner. When Carter and Mitch started their ad agency fresh from college, Simon had quickly followed suit, using his parents' money to gain some of the best clients around. But a year later, it was Kovich & Edwards Agency that had come out on top. Mitch and Carter had been a dream team, with Carter's business head and Mitchell's ability to spot artistic talent. Not to mention, both of them knew how to treat a client like they were king. The next few years, client after client had left Thomas Ad Agency and signed on with K&E, most of them claiming that lack of communication and the difficulty of working with Simon were the main reasons.

He didn't want Simon Thomas anywhere near Eve, professionally or personally, let alone have her sign on as partner with Thomas Ad Agency.

Carter had looked at Eve's proposal the first night she'd handed it to him and Mitch. He'd spent the whole night reading it over and had an emergency meeting with Mitch the next morning. They would have been stupid not to accept her offer. After all, she was one of the reasons their business had grown so much since they'd brought her on nearly five years ago.

He rested for the remainder of the short trip to Chicago and thought about their dinner plans. The only reason he'd put off making Eve partner was the little leverage he'd had over her. He wasn't a control freak, but he liked knowing she had to come to him for some of the decisions she made. When she was full partner, he'd miss that. But he couldn't deny that she deserved the spot. Nor could he deny the attraction he felt for her or the fact that he'd been building up to trying to ask her out. He'd broken up with Lisa, his last girlfriend, only five months ago. It hadn't been one of his longest relationships, only lasting three months. He found it hard to maintain interested in someone ten years his junior when all they wanted to talk about was shopping. He'd called the relationship off, and he'd realized after seeing Mitch and Sandi together that it was time he stepped up and tried for the person he'd always wanted, even if it meant putting himself out there and getting rejected.

His relationship with Eve hadn't always been smooth. A lot of times, they would end their meetings in a fight, usually with Eve winning. The woman knew more tricks to get what she wanted and seemed to always play him for the fool. Not that he minded. Half the time she'd use her sexy hazel eyes on him and he'd lose all his steam. He did enjoy their bantering, often thinking days ahead of how he could win a little tiff he knew was on the way.

He thought about her sitting next to him now and frowned a little. He really had wanted to tell her about the agreement over dinner but hearing her plans with Simon had forced him to play his hand early.

When he felt the plane start to descend, he opened his eyes and found her reading over the agreement he'd had the lawyers draw up. There was a slight frown on her face and a small crinkle between her eyes. She always got that look when she was unhappy about something. She was too busy reading to notice his assessment of her. Her long chestnut hair was tied up in a smart-looking knot at the nape of her neck. Her dark slacks and cream-colored shirt showcased her curvy figure and beautiful olive skin. He and Mitchell always called her Greek Goddess behind her back and the term rang true. But the fact that she could hold her own in a boardroom and sweet talk most clients into anything, gave her the upper edge in his book.

He concentrated on her ear as she read. Her little silver ball earrings bounced as the plane bumped as it landed. She was so caught up in reading, she didn't freak out as she normally did when a plane was landing.

"You took that one like a pro." He chuckled.

"Hmmm, what?" She looked over at him.

"The landing. You didn't freak out." He watched fear come into her eyes as she looked around.

"We've landed?" Upon seeing her grip, the folder tightly, he laughed.

It took a little over an hour to get out of O'Hare and into a taxi heading to their hotel downtown. It was just after noon, so the traffic set them back another hour. He knew she wanted to talk about the paperwork and was surprised that she didn't bring it up. Instead, she looked out the window in deep thought. He had a few loose ends to tie up on his phone and stayed busy most of the taxi ride.

When they arrived at the hotel, Eve checked in and then waited for him in the lobby. He could tell she was deep in thought because when they started walking towards the elevators, he threw her bag over his shoulder and she didn't object. He'd known her since the fourth grade, and she'd never allowed anyone to carry anything for her or to even open the door for her. She was very independent and made sure to let everyone know she could take care of herself.

He supposed it stemmed from being raised by her father. Eve came from a very strict military family. Her father was commanding officer at Fort Drum, a base in upstate New York. Eve never really had anyone to watch out for her. Even now, her family didn't really have a lot to do with her life. Even when they were kids, Eve had pretty much been on her own. He supposed that's why he and Mitch had become such close friends with her. The three of them were pretty much left to their own devices growing up.

Carter was the only one out of the bunch that had family, but after his grandparents died, that had gone away. His mother and father had divorced when Carter was young. He could only remember seeing his dad a handful of times. His mother had always been off somewhere. She'd been in South Africa helping towns build wells when she'd gotten sick. He loved that his mom had such a big heart. He just wished she would have used it closer to home a little more often.

But he'd had his friends and that's all he'd ever needed. Even now, holidays were spent with them, a tradition they'd started in high school. It was just common knowledge that no matter where they were, they'd come together and be there for one another.

He smiled at Eve as they entered the elevator. She'd been like a sister to him, until she hadn't. He supposed it was all his fault, really. That kiss had been rolling around in his head for years before he'd acted on it. Since then, their relationship had changed. Not by much, but things were different. He couldn't really put his finger on it, but the sexual tension had tripled between them, especially after her break up with Steve. He knew she'd tried dating shortly after the breakup, each time ending badly. She'd come to her friends for support, and eventually turned to her work to fill the emptiness. A lot like he'd done over the course of the years while she'd been engaged.

He'd tried dating as well. Lisa, for example. Each time had ended just as badly as Eve's relationships had. Actually, now that he thought about it, this was the first time they were both single at the same time.

He watched Eve as she chewed her bottom lip and knew she had something on her mind. "What?" He leaned against the elevator wall.

"What?" She looked at him, trying to fake innocence in her eyes.

"You can't pretend nothing is on your mind. You're dying to get something off your chest." The elevator door opened on their floor. He picked up their bags and they walked out together. He'd arranged it so his room was right next to hers, so when she entered her door, he tried to follow her in.

She slapped her arm across the door and glared at him. "I can take it from here." She held out her hand for her bag.

"I know you can but seeing as you have something you want to get off your chest, we might as well hash it out now." She looked at him and he could see her change her mind, her eyes soften a little. Smiling, he ducked under her arm and walked into her room and set her bag down.

CHAPTER 2

$\mathcal{E}$ ve watched Carter walk in and felt her heart flutter. She was nervous. It was stupid of her, but she was nervous. This was someone she'd always known, had been best friends with forever, yet she didn't know how to say what she wanted. She hated feeling this way.

So she took her time closing the door and setting down her purse and briefcase. When she looked, he'd made himself comfortable on the couch by the window, his suitcase and bag lying on the floor next to him. She removed her coat and sat across from him at the table. Her hands were sweaty, and she really wished Mitch was here as well.

"I've looked over the paperwork." She took out the large stack of papers he'd given her on the plane. "And I think everything looks good, with the exception of a few items."

Carter leaned forward, his elbows on his knees as he waited.

"I'd like to stick with my initial buy-in price." She held

her breath. Her buy-in was important to her. It secured her spot as an equal partner in the agency, something she demanded. The paperwork he'd given her had a much lower buy-in rate. She was determined to win this argument.

"It's not necessary. Mitch agreed with me on the amount and the lawyers have already drawn up the paperwork." He leaned back and crossed his foot over his knee.

Taking a deep breath, she tilted her head and looked at him. "Carter, you know as well as I do that paperwork can be changed. My buy-in amount stays the same."

He smiled and shook his head. She knew another way to get his opinion to change and decided to pull out her ace. "There is one more item I'd like to discuss."

He waved his hand for her to continue.

"I'd like to change the name from Kovich & Edwards Agency." She bit her lip waiting for the explosion she knew was coming. It was an old conversation they'd had many arguments over. Mitch had even taken her side at one point.

"What?" He jumped from the couch and walked towards her. "You've got to be joking." He looked down at her and she saw the humor that was there a few seconds ago had drained from his eyes.

"No. I think we need to bring the agency into this century. Using last names is very old-fashioned." She crossed her legs and watched him get even more flustered. She knew how to control his moods, just like she knew how to play Mitchell and all of her clients. Carter was a lot easier since he was easily distracted. All she had to do was lick her lips or cross her legs, and he'd lose his thoughts.

"What do you suggest?" His teeth were clenched as he leaned closer to her, his hands on the table in front of her.

"Well, I've been suggesting Creative Ad Agency for years. Now that we are making a major change by adding me on as a partner, I see no reason not to go through with the name change as well." She smiled a little.

He leaned closer to her. "Ever since you first mentioned it, I've made it clear how I felt." He was so close that she could see the light dusting of freckles on his nose. She smiled and relaxed back in her chair. "Choose. I will have one or the other."

He stood up and threw his hands in the air.

"Then it's settled. My buy-in amount changes and the agency name will remain the same." She handed him back the paperwork.

He took the stack of papers and picked up his bags, then walked to the door. "I have a feeling you got exactly what you wanted." He walked out without another word and even though she'd gotten everything, there was an empty spot in her chest.

Later that evening, after she'd showered and dressed for dinner, there was a knock on her door. When she'd opened it she'd expected to see Carter, but instead, Simon Thomas stood outside her door in a very expensive suit. The smell of his cologne hit her like a brick wall and she almost gagged on the musky scent.

"Oh, I'm sorry, Simon. I'm afraid I had to cancel our dinner tonight. I left a message with your secretary." She said, then bit her lip.

Simon Thomas was tall, had wonderful blond, curly hair and piercing blue eyes. He looked like the all-American boy from next door, but she knew he had a mean streak in him. She'd heard all about it from some of his ex-clients that she'd signed on to K&E. Still, their business relationship was hanging by threads and she didn't want to burn any bridges she might have to cross later on.

"I received your message. Pam is a very efficient secretary." He walked past her into her room without her invitation. She stood in the doorway, her hand still on the doorknob, trying to figure out how to get him out of her hair. "I thought maybe you'd change your mind again. I know how women are, always saying one thing and then regretting it. Besides, I really wanted to talk to you about…"

There was a cough behind her, causing her to jump. She spun around and saw Carter leaning against the door jam. "I didn't mean to interrupt; I must be coming down with a cold." Carter cleared his throat again and walked in.

Now she had two uninvited guests in her room. She leaned against the door, knowing it wasn't going to be a pretty scene.

"Simon." Carter nodded his head and held out his hand. Simon had a look on his face like he'd smelled something foul, but then he shook Carter's hand. Eve could see the men struggle to overpower each other with firm grips.

"I'm sorry, Simon. I've made other plans tonight." She tried to paste a sincere smile on her face. Truthfully, she just wanted to curl up and study her notes for tomorrow's meeting with Tom Russell. She really needed this client and didn't want to go anywhere that would take her mind off tomorrow's big meeting.

"Yes, I can see that." Simon walked towards the door. "If you change your mind about meeting with me while you're in town, you know how to reach me." Simon nodded towards Carter and then walked out the door.

Eve gently shut the door behind him and leaned her back against it. "Well, that went better than I thought it would."

Carter laughed. "Yeah. Well, what you need now is some beer and pizza. Shall we go?"

"Listen, Carter. I think I'll just order in. I've got a few things I need to go over before tomorrow's meeting." She started walking towards the table and her laptop.

"Oh no." He grabbed her arm and steered her towards the door, picking up her purse and coat as they walked by them. "You are not making any lame excuses to me. I promised you pizza and beer and I'm going to deliver. Besides, I thought we were celebrating our new partnership."

She allowed him to help her on with her coat and grabbed her purse from him. "Fine, one beer and a slice of pizza. Then I need to get back here so I can catch up before the meeting."

"Good." He smiled and held her arm as they walked out together.

Carter was right, what she needed was a beer and pizza. Not to mention laughter. Carter was really entertaining when he put his mind to it. Sitting across from him in the dark booth, a large slice of some of the best cheese pizza she'd ever had in her hand, she remembered why she thought of him as one of her best friends.

She remembered all the fun times they had with Mitchell, the three of them growing up together. All the laughter. Even some of the arguments she looked back on fondly. Carter and Mitchell are what mattered most to her.

Every time she thought about heading back to the hotel, Carter would order another drink for her. Finally, just after midnight, she pushed her empty glass away and kicked him under the table when he tried to order another drink for her.

As they were walking out, he grabbed hold of her arm to steady her and she leaned against him for support. She didn't usually drink this much and the feel of his arm around her caused her to let her guard down for a while. They walked back to their hotel, which was only a few blocks away, with her leaning heavily on him.

The chill in the air caused her to pull her coat closer, and she could see her breath in the night air. "I always liked this time of year up here. It reminds me of visiting your grandparents' place for Christmas." She looked at the row of lights that lined the street. If she squinted, she could just imagine them as Christmas lights, lining the road.

"I miss your grandparents." She sighed and leaned her head against his shoulder. When he wrapped his arm around her more tightly, she closed her eyes for a second.

"Hmm. Me, too. Do you remember the last time we were all up there together?"

"Yes, the party." She stopped and turned to look at him. His face was shadowed in the street light that shined behind his head. "The kiss." She looked at his lips now and wondered if it would feel as good now as it had then. Maybe she'd built it up in her mind over the years? Maybe he wasn't as great of a kisser as she remembered?

She hadn't realized that she'd leaned into him until his arms came around her shoulders.

"Yeah, I've been meaning to talk to you about that." He

frowned a little and she watched his mouth, thinking of how soft his lips would feel next to hers.

"Did you ever notice that we talk too much about everything?" She wrapped her arms around his neck and pulled him down to her.

She was right; his lips were soft and warm and felt like heaven. She moaned and pushed her hands through his thick hair. His hands flexed on her hips before they journeyed up her back as he pulled her closer. She could feel his heart beat against her chest and mentally cursed the layer of clothing between them.

"Eve?" Carter pulled back and rested his head on her forehead. "It's starting to rain."

"Mmm." She looked up into the dark sky and realized she felt alive. Pulling away from him, she did a quick spin, only to end up back in his arms when she almost toppled over. She was laughing as she looked up into his face. "I like the rain. I like Chicago. I like kissing you. Can we do it again?"

He laughed and pulled her along the sidewalk. "Sure, let's get out of the cold first."

She walked next to him and at several points along the short walk even closed her eyes as she leaned against him.

When they walked into the lobby of the hotel, the warmth hit her and she felt a little steadier on her feet. Her mind kicked into gear and when she got into the elevator, she stood with her back against the wall as Carter hit the buttons. She closed her eyes, leaned her head against the cool glass, and took a couple deep breaths.

"Eve?" When she opened her eyes, Carter was standing right in front of her. "I can see you're already regretting the kiss." He smiled down at her.

She shook her head lightly. "Not regretting, just questioning."

"Questioning what?" He moved closer and put his hands on her hips, pulling her up and closer to him. When he touched her, it was like her brain refused to think again.

"You. Me." She looked at his mouth. Somehow, now, it was worse knowing what he could do to her with his mouth. Why did he have to be so good at kissing?

"I thought you said we think too much?" He leaned towards her, stopping just before their lips met, giving her time to pull away or say no. She didn't want to say no. She wanted to go on kissing him, feeling his hands on her. When his mouth touched hers, she moaned and relaxed into the feeling of him kissing her thoroughly. Somehow, her back ended up against the wall again as his hands roamed over and under her coat. Silently cursing all the layers between them again, she plunged her hands into his wet hair, enjoying the softness.

He pulled back and smiled at her as the elevator doors opened. Then he took her hand and they walked towards their rooms. When they got to her door, he leaned down and kissed her again. She fumbled for the door, trying to open it. He pulled back and laughed, and taking her key card from her hand, he smoothly opened her door. But when she moved to pull him inside her room, he frowned and shook his head.

"Better not. We've got time to think about things. Besides, we have an early meeting and it's late. Get some sleep." He leaned down and kissed her frowning lips. "I'll see you in the morning." He walked to the door next to hers and looked back at her after he opened it. "Go inside." He smiled at her.

She had been standing there watching him and realized he wouldn't go into his room until she was safely in her own for the night. Still frowning, she shut her door and leaned against it, closing her eyes. She was in trouble. She knew it. She also knew that there was no way she was going to not kiss Carter again.

The next morning Carter knocked on Eve's hotel door at precisely seven o'clock. He made sure to knock loudly enough, just in case she had overslept. But when she opened the door, fully dressed, with a cup of coffee in her hands, his mood sank a little.

She smiled. "Remember, I never have hangovers." She motioned for him to enter. "I got an extra plate of toast and there's some coffee left if you want."

He walked into her room, his head hanging in disappointment. He was at least hoping that she'd had a hard time sleeping last night like he had. It had taken him almost two hours to fall asleep; he just couldn't stop thinking about her. Even in his dreams, she had been there.

He set his briefcase down and walked over to the small table and sat. Watching her pour him a cup of coffee, he smiled as she added the right amount of cream to his cup. He liked knowing that she remembered how he took his coffee. He admired her slender form and the way her black dress pants fit her. Her sexy high heels gave her a few inches, so they almost stood eye to eye. The cream-colored blouse looked almost see-through, but he knew she'd ruin the sexy look by covering up with the blazer that was hanging on the back of her chair. Her long, dark hair was tied in a fancy-looking knot at the base of her neck, with little curly wisps of hair around her face, accenting her exotic features. With her dark skin, she always looked like she'd just walked off the beach. Her large hazel eyes, in Carter's opinion, were her best feature. They seemed to tell her whole story, even when she didn't want them to. He could tell when she was playing him or when she was sad, angry, or hurt. It was one of the main reasons he had grown to feel the way he did about her. Most women he'd trusted had ended up hurting him. With Eve he knew where he stood, and he knew that she'd never do anything intentionally to damage their relationship.

"So…what is your strategy for today's meeting?" He asked, then leaned back and listened to her talk about her plans to gain another client. He knew without a doubt that she was the best at winning people over.

An hour later, he watched Eve work her magic with Tom Russell. She was smooth in getting him to sign on as K&E's next biggest talent. The two-hundred-pound foot-ball player was no match for Eve's charm. Carter had never seen such a huge man smile and laugh as hard as Tom had in their hour-long meeting. When Eve pulled out her paperwork, Tom signed without even reading through the stack of documents.

As they walked out of the building, Carter took Eve's hand casually. "Well done, partner. What do you say to some lunch?" He felt Eve's hand tense a little, but then she sighed and her hand relaxed in his.

"Sure, but only if you're buying. And no pizza." She smiled.

CHAPTER 3

$\mathcal{E}$ ve sat across from Carter feeling a little tired. Negotiations always seemed to suck all the energy out of her. After the waitress poured her coffee, she took a large sip and closed her eyes. She hadn't realized she was rubbing her forehead until Carter said something to her.

"Headache? You look tired all of a sudden." Carter took a sip of his coffee and watched her from across the table.

"No and yes. No headache, just a little twinge. Yes, to the other part. You would think that after a successful meeting, I'd be pumped, but instead, I'm always a little drained. I usually find a corner to collect myself after negotiations, and then when I feel better, I find some way of celebrating." She tried to paste on her best smile. She hated that Carter could see her weaknesses. He and Mitchell had always seen all her weaknesses. Maybe that's why they were such good friends because neither of them ever exploited her. After knowing the two of them most of her life, she knew their weaknesses, as well. It was nice having people around you that made you feel like home. Carter and Mitchell were just that to her—home.

But after last night, her feelings and thoughts about Carter had started to change. Well, if she was honest with herself, her feelings and thoughts about him had started to change a while back. She always enjoyed the little tiffs they had. But lately, there were other emotions brewing underneath. She tried to hide them from not only him, but also herself.

She'd had some pretty detailed dreams last night after he'd walked away from her. She'd tried falling straight asleep, but instead, she'd listened, hoping for some sound from the next room, where he was staying.

"Well," Carter said, interrupting her thoughts, "maybe we can head back to the hotel and you can gather yourself. Then, later, we can head to this great pub I know. They have really great food and live music."

She thought about it and realized it sounded great. She'd always loved coming to Chicago but had never really had anyone to show her around before. She'd stuck close to her hotel and never really ventured out by herself. Having Carter along was perfect.

At seven thirty that evening, Carter knocked on her door. Before opening it, she took one last look at her reflection. The tight burgundy dress was sure to knock his socks off. She imagined his chin hitting the floor and his eyes bulging out like they did in the cartoons. His heart would beat out of his chest and he'd fall at her feet. She'd brought the dress along hoping to wear it during her meeting with Simon Thomas. After all, she wanted to leave an impression, just in case. It never hurt to have another option for business lined up. Now, however, she wasn't thinking of business but pleasure. She smiled, thinking of kissing Carter again, as she slid on some lipstick and walked over to open the door. The look on Carter's face was priceless. Smiling, even more, she looked at him from head to toe. He was wearing dark dress pants and a light gray shirt. He carried his leather jacket in one hand and had a single white long-stemmed rose in the other. The rose hung by his side, forgotten.

"You look…wow." He smiled at her. "Wonderful."

She reached down and took the rose from his fingertips. "Thank you. You're not bad yourself."

Turning slowly, she walked back into the room, grabbed a glass and filled it with water for the rose. When she turned towards Carter, he was standing just inside the doorway, watching her. She could see the heat in his eyes, which caused a strange flutter in her chest.

For a split second, she thought about celebrating here in her hotel room instead of in some noisy, crowded pub. She could just imagine them ripping off each other's clothes, tearing up the sheets. Then she shook her head clear and grabbed her coat as Carter walked over and helped her. She'd left her hair down, and when she started to pull her hair out from under the coat, he reached up and helped. He stood behind her, his hands in her hair and she could hear him breathing. His hands remained in her hair a little longer and she enjoyed the feeling of him touching her. When she turned around, he was looking at her as if he was trying to decide something.

"Are you sure we can't find some way to celebrate here?" He reached out and gently ran his fingers over her cheek. She tried to level her breathing but found it harder and harder to steady herself. She slowly shook her head no, not really meaning it, not sure if she could control herself for much longer.

"No, I'm ready for some loud music, and you promised me food." Her voice hitched.

The taxi ride seemed to take forever. The Friday night traffic was not only slowing them down but also making things steam up in the back seat. Every turn the cab made caused Carter's knee to rub up against hers. She felt the heat from him radiating up her legs, heading straight to her core. She'd always thought she was in control of her sex drive, but by the time they stopped in front of Brian's Pub, she wanted nothing more than to rush back to the hotel and jump him.

Then the taxi door opened, and the cold air hit her, helping clear her head and hormones. They walked into the pub, which was wonderfully noisy and crowded. There was a band playing on a small stage in the back corner. She'd always loved the sound of electric violins like the ones that the two women in the band were playing now. She enjoyed the sound as they walked across the room looking for a place to sit. Finally, Carter found a small booth across from the stage and when they sat, she tried to avoid looking at him by glancing down at the menu instead.

"Do they really serve green beer?" She looked up from her menu at Carter.

He nodded and smiled, then nodded across the room. Looking across the room, she saw a man taking a drink of green liquid from a large glass mug.

"Yes, you'll have to try some. They have wonderful shepherd's pie here as well." He waved the waitress down and they both ordered green beer and shepherd's pie, chicken for him, vegan for her.

The music slowed down and the whole room seemed to get quiet. When the violins started playing this time, she was completely consumed with the sadness of the sound.

By the time the song ended, their food was being delivered. While they ate, they talked about the meeting and about several of Eve's thoughts and plans for K&E's future.

They were interrupted when the song turned fast and the two female violinists climbed up on tables across the room from each other. A violin duel began between the tall blonde, who was across the room and the short dark-haired woman who happened to be standing on their table. The two women played back and forth, each taking their turn giving everything they had to the fast-paced music. Eve could see a bead of sweat rolling down the dark-haired woman's brow when the song finally finished. Carter helped her climbed off their table and was rewarded with a kiss on his cheek, which caused the crowd to cheer. When he sat down, Eve laughed and smiled at him as the violinist walked back towards the small stage area.

By the time Eve ordered her second green beer for the evening, she was feeling light-hearted and was dead set on getting Carter on the dance floor.

She loved dancing but hadn't been to a nightclub in years, not since her friend Dana's bachelorette party last year. She knew both Carter and Mitchell hated dancing, which was one of the main reasons she'd never gone clubbing with either of them. By the time she dragged Carter to the dance floor, an hour later, they were both laughing and enjoying themselves so much.

It was much later, when they left the bar, that she leaned heavily on him, again. Déjà vu played in her head, but this time, she knew how she wanted the evening to end. He didn't have any excuses tonight. No early morning meetings that they had to go to. Their flight didn't leave until later tomorrow afternoon, so that wasn't an issue either.

"Damn!" Carter exclaimed when they were a few feet from the door. Searching his pockets and frowning. "I left my cell phone in the booth." He pulled away. "I'll be right back." He kissed her quickly and disappeared back into the pub while she leaned against a light pole, smiling at him.

Carter was relieved that his phone was still there, stuck between the booth's cushions. He rushed through the growing crowd and back out the front door, expecting to see Eve leaning against the light pole or a wall, but she was nowhere to be found. Fear hit him full force, causing adrenaline to rush to every pore of his body.

Had she gone back inside? He looked around. There were a few other people coming and going outside the pub, and he asked a few of them as they walked by if they'd seen her, but they all said no. He knew she wouldn't have taken a cab without him. He looked everywhere. Just as he was about to walk back into the building, he heard a scream.

Rushing to the end of the street, he turned down an alley. It looked like one of those alleys you see on all the movies: darker than the streets, lined with huge trash bins that consumed the narrow way. The scream had been like a shot in the night. He wasn't even sure which direction it had come from.

"Hey man? What are you looking for?" There were two young men, dressed in fatigues. Each had a pretty girl on their arm.

"Eve." He said just her name. "She's about this tall, dark hair, wearing a dark jacket, a dark dress."

"We haven't seen her. But we both heard a scream." While the two girls hung back, the three men walked cautiously into the alley. One of the marines pulled out a small flashlight as they all looked around.

"Carrie said the scream came from down here," the one with the light said, while he searched around the dumpsters.

"Eve?" Carter called out over and over. "I just left her for a second. I forgot my cell phone inside."

"Here, over here," the young marine without the light screamed. "Oh man." Carter watched him step back and cover his mouth with his hand in horror.

Carter rushed over to where the man stood over Eve. Her coat was ripped, her dark hair fanned out over her face, so he couldn't see if she was alive. When he knelt beside her, he slowly moved her wet hair away from her face with shaky fingers. Just let her be alive, he prayed.

"I'm calling 911," someone said behind him. Carter felt for a pulse with shaky fingers and found a weak one. He let out a sigh and pulled Eve up into his lap gently. His hand came away from her head wet, and when he looked, it was covered with blood. The red fluid shone in the light of the flashlight.

"She's bleeding." This time it was one of the girls that

stood behind him. "I'm a nurse. You shouldn't move her." She bent down on Eve's other side.

"I…I'm sorry." He looked up into the young woman's face. "I left her for just a second." He repeated not knowing that tears had fogged his vision.

"It's okay. Here," The woman took off her jacket and laid it on the ground. "Rest her back on this. We need to keep her still until the ambulance gets here. My name's Beth. I'm going to need you to hold this over her wound." She held out a white handkerchief.

"I didn't think anyone carried handkerchiefs anymore." It was a stupid thing to say, and he realized then that he was probably in shock.

Beth laughed and put the cloth in his hand and held his hand over a large gash on the side of Eve's head.

"Don't be afraid to put a little pressure on it. We have to stop the bleeding. I'm going to make sure she isn't hurt anywhere else." Beth started running her hands over Eve's unconscious body. Carter looked at Eve's face and felt a tear slide down his cheek. How could he have been so stupid as to leave her alone?

"It's Bobbie's," Beth looked at him and smiled. "The handkerchief." She nodded towards the marine with the flashlight, who was shining the light over Eve so Beth could examine her. In the distance, Carter heard the sirens. What was taking them so long? "The handkerchief is Bobbie's," Beth repeated and smiled up at her date. "He always tells me to be prepared for everything. Your wife doesn't have any more injuries that I can see. Just the nasty bump and cut on her head. She might have a sprained wrist." Beth held Eve's arm up and Carter could see the bruises forming on her pale skin where her coat sleeve had ripped.

Carter flashed from fear to anger so quickly. Someone had done this to her. Someone had attacked her, and he hadn't been there to protect her. It was all his fault.

An hour later, at the hospital, he sat next to Eve, who was still unconscious. The doctors and nurses had come and gone. One stood over her, prepping her for a CAT scan. The police had come and were now outside the small room talking to Bobbie, Beth, Carrie, and Frank, the two marines and their dates, who had followed behind the ambulance to make sure everything was all right. So far, Carter had yet to regain his wits. Every time the police asked him a question, he would just repeat his story, and when he got to the point of leaving Eve on the curb to go back and retrieve his cell, he would choke up.

His head hurt, his eyes were dry and scratchy, and he knew he needed rest like everyone had been telling him. At this point, he didn't give a damn. He refused to leave her side when they rolled her in to examine her. Finally, the nurses just pulled the curtain and let him stand behind it in the same room. When they started to roll Eve out to take her upstairs to get a CAT scan, he held onto her bed and followed.

"I'm sorry, Mr. Edwards. You can't come in this room," a short, plump nurse said. She had a friendly face, but upon hearing this news, he thought of her as evil. Then she smiled and pointed to a small glass area. "You can stay in there with the technician, though. We normally don't allow it, but for you, we'll make an exception. Just go through that door." She pointed, and he slowly let go of the bed. Then he pulled the bed to a stop as the nurse looked at him. He leaned over Eve and whispered into her ear, then kissed her gently on the lips. When he stood, the nurse was smiling at him. He turned and walked into the small glass room, watching as the nurse and technician transferred Eve's unconscious body onto the bed for the scan.

The scan took longer than he imagined it would. By the time the machines had come to a stop, his head was drooping. When the nurse showed up to take Eve back to a private room, she had a cup of coffee in her hands. "I thought you might need this."

"Thank you." He gulped the lukewarm liquid down in two swallows. He could feel the caffeine instantly shooting through his system, reviving him. They walked by a small waiting area. He could see the two couples still sitting on the benches there.

"I'm Laura. If you need anything…" The nurse pushed Eve's bed back into the private room and locked the wheels. "We should know something soon. If you don't mind, the two couples that helped you would like to talk to you."

He nodded and pulled a chair closer to Eve's bed. Reaching down, he grabbed her hand. It was cool and soft and looked very small in his. Her normally dark skin had a pale tint to it. He rubbed her hand, trying to get the color and warmth back into her fingers.

"Hey," Bobbie said as the four of them walked into the room. "How's she doing?"

He shook his head. "They aren't sure." He looked back down at Eve. A large white bandage covered most of her head. Her hair had been pushed aside and had been cut around the large gash. He knew she was very particular about her hair and probably wouldn't like that someone had hacked a good chunk off her head. Her face looked even paler than her hands.

"Head wounds always seem worse than they are." Beth walked forward and rested her hands on the bed. "A bump like that might take some time to heal. She was lucky. She didn't lose too much blood." When he just looked at the young woman, she continued. "Head wounds bleed a lot. I think we stopped the bleeding quickly. Whoever attacked her, the scream must have scared them off." She looked at the other three people in the room.

"At least that's what we think." Bobbie stepped forward and put a hand on Beth's shoulder. "We told the police everything we could. I wanted to give you my number. I'm stationed just outside of town. I'd appreciate an update on your wife. We're all very concerned." The four of them looked at him and for the first time, he realized how kind these strangers were being. Emotions flooded him and almost overpowered him, causing tears to slip down his face for the second time that night.

Carter stood and held out his hand towards Bobbie. "I can't thank you guys enough. I'm glad you were there to help out. I know Eve"—he looked back down at her on the bed, unmoving— "would know what to say, she would have the right words." He choked up as Bobbie shook his hand.

"It's okay, man. I know how you must feel. I lost several of my unit in Iraq a few years back."

Carter balked. "A few years back? How old are you? You can't be over nineteen."

Bobbie laughed. "I'm twenty-two. I was eighteen at the time and thought I knew and had seen it all when our

Hummer was hit." He looked at Beth. "That's when we met." He pulled her closer as they smiled at each other.

"You should have heard him complaining. Some shrapnel to his shoulder and he turns into a little girl," Beth said, smiling up at Bobbie.

"We'd all like to know how your wife does. Just give me a call anytime." They shook his hand again as Carter nodded his head. Bobbie handed him a piece of paper with his cell number on it. Carter tucked it into his wallet.

After the four of them left, Carter sat back for a long night. Laura and several other nurses came and went over the next few hours. Each time they came in, he would awaken in his spot in the chair next to Eve.

When he noticed the light coming through the windows, he took out his cell phone. He had a few calls he knew he couldn't put off any longer.

The first call was to Mitchell, who promised to have their flight and hotel taken care of. Then he told him he and Sandi would be on the next flight to Chicago themselves and to expect them after lunch.

The next call was to Eve's parents. The colonel wasn't available, so he left a message with his secretary who promised to pass on the information as soon as the colonel was back in the States.

He tried to call Eve's mother, but when he dialed the number he had for her, he was told it was disconnected. He sat back down when the nurses came in to check on her again. So far, she hadn't moved a muscle. He'd tried several times during the night to wake her by gently rubbing her hand and arm.

Her left arm was in a large white splint. They'd told him after they took x-rays that it was just sprained. Her sexy dress had been cut off her; her coat had been ruined as well. He stood over her, not knowing what to do.

"I brought you some breakfast," Laura said, carrying a large tray in and setting it on the stand. "There's some coffee and orange juice. If you want anything different, just let the new nurse on staff know." She smiled and wheeled the cart towards a chair. "Come, sit." She motioned to the chair. He walked over and sat down so she could push the cart up to him. "I'm getting off shift now, but the day nurse will take care of you. If you're still here tonight, I'll be back around eleven." She walked over to Eve and checked her vitals.

"Any change?" he asked, taking a sip of the hospital coffee.

Laura shook her head no. "But that's neither good nor bad. We'll just have to wait this out." She smiled at him. "Have you contacted your families?"

He nodded his head and opened the lid to his food. There were toast, eggs, bacon, and biscuits with jelly. He doubted he could eat anything, but after Laura left, he started nibbling. When he looked down again, his plate was empty. Pushing it aside, he walked back to the window and looked out. Snow had started falling and from the tenth floor, everything looked peaceful and beautiful.

CHAPTER 4

He didn't know how long he'd stood there, looking at the city, but sometime later, he heard the door open and close. Turning, he saw Mitchell and Sandi standing just inside the door. He felt relieved that his friends were there.

The next days were a blur. He refused to leave Eve's room and it wasn't until Mitch pulled him aside and told him he stunk that he went into the small bathroom and jumped in the shower, only to put on the same clothes he'd been wearing before. At least he was clean and felt a little more human. When he'd walked out of the bathroom, Mitch had just shaken his head at him. He knew his friend wasn't going to push him into returning to the hotel. He'd made it very clear that he wasn't leaving.

"I can get you a change of clothes in the morning. Just give me your hotel key." Sandi smiled at him.

Before he could respond, he heard a moan and rushed to Eve's side just as her eyes fluttered open.

He could see she was confused when he looked into

her unfocused eyes. Then the doctor was pushing them from the room, and Carter was following Mitch and Sandi down the hall towards the elevators.

She was awake, Carter kept telling himself over and over as he stood in the elevator heading down to the cafeteria.

The first night Mitch had been there, he'd sat up with Carter in Eve's room. Carter could tell that Mitch knew something was up between him and Eve. He knew his friend was dying to ask, so instead of waiting, Carter had blurted out that he loved her. Mitch's response was a huge smile.

"Well, it's about time." His friend had shocked him; he didn't know what to say. Then Mitch had asked. "Does she feel the same way?"

"I…I don't know. We were just about to…" Carter had closed his eyes and rested his head in his hands.

Now, as they sat in the cafeteria, his friend was sitting next to his fiancée and was looking so much in love. Sandi had been a blessing to Mitch. Ever since Mitch's ex had broken him, he'd been a wreck. Then Sandi had come into his life and Carter could see the changes in his friend. Mitch actually smiled more.

Looking across the table at the small woman that had healed his friend, he noticed how opposite they were. Mitch was blond with green eyes and pale skin. Sandi, coming from the Middle East, had darker skin and rich dark eyes. She was shorter and smaller than Eve, not to mention a good ten years younger than the three of them.

Carter knew that Sandi had gone through so much in the past few years—running from her family, her life hanging in the balance, then losing her father and cousin.

He couldn't imagine the horror she'd endured last year when her cousin had almost killed her, killing her father instead. He closed his eyes as an image of Eve flashed in his mind, of her lying on the ground in the alley.

"Hey, man?" Mitch broke into his thoughts. "Don't worry. The worst is over." Mitch slapped him on the shoulder.

"Yeah," he looked across at his friend. "I know you're right."

"Have you thought about what you're going to do?" Sandi asked.

"What do you mean?" He sipped the coffee Sandi set in front of him.

Sandi looked between the two men. "Really?" She shook her head and chuckled a little. "Eve is going to need some time to recover. She'll need to stay somewhere, with someone."

Carter hadn't thought of that. Would Eve need some recovery time? An image of his grandparents' house flashed in his mind. He'd been meaning to get up there and take care of some home improvement projects that needed to be done. It had sat empty ever since Mitch and Sandi had stayed there last year, hiding out.

"Eve? I don't think she'll want to take much time. We know her too well. She'll probably want to get back to work tomorrow." Mitch laughed and drank his iced tea.

Carter thought about it and knew his friend was right. She was probably up there arguing with the doctor about leaving the hospital right now.

When they went back upstairs, the doctor was standing outside Eve's room, talking quietly with a nurse. As they approached, he walked towards them. "I'd like to speak to you privately. We can use an office down here." He motioned for them to follow him.

When they were all seated in the small space, the doctor stood in front of the desk. "I'm afraid the bump to Miss Taylor's head was a little more severe than we thought. Her CAT scans were clean and there are no signs of permanent damage." He held up his hands, trying to assure them. "But the bump to her head has given her a case of amnesia. It's hard to say if it's temporary or long-term. I've seen cases like this where the memory loss lasts only a few hours, but there are cases where something like this is permanent."

Carter stood, and his entire body shook. "Eve can't remember anything?" When the doctor shook his head, Carter rushed from the room, leaving his friends and the doctor to finish talking.

When Carter entered Eve's room, she was sitting up, talking to a nurse. When Eve saw him, she smiled, and for a split second, he thought that the doctor had played a nasty trick on him. Then he got a better look at her eyes and he could see the smile she was giving him was the same kind of smile she'd always given clients she'd just met. The sparkle didn't flash in her eyes. His shoulders sank along with his heart.

When the group of people came back in, Eve watched as each of them looked at her like she'd just been given a week to live. Shock and sadness crossed every face. After a few minutes, she couldn't take it anymore and asked the nurse if she could go to the restroom. The young woman helped her walk into the bathroom, showing her how to pull the emergency cord if she needed any help.

When she shut the door, she made sure to lock it as she leaned back and closed her eyes. Her head hurt, her wrist hurt, and she had never felt so alone. She didn't want anyone's pity. Especially since she couldn't remember the people who were standing around her hospital bed as if they belonged there. Like they had no plans to leave any time soon.

When she opened her eyes and started walking across the small space, she noticed movement out of the corner of her eye. Looking, she saw her reflection for the first time in her memory. Her eyesight was still fuzzy, so she stepped closer to the mirror and leaned on the sink to get a better look.

She had rich olive skin and large hazel eyes that looked a little hollow at the moment. There were dark circles under them and she could see a large bruise on her left temple just underneath a white bandage that sat over long, dark chestnut hair. The hospital gown hung loosely on a curvy figure. She looked down at her toes and memorized the shape of each one. Her nails were painted a deep red. Looking at her hands, she noticed long fingers with neat, clean fingernails painted the same color. Her left arm was in a sling and she tried not to move it too much. Her left ribs and back ached when she twisted or moved fast.

Looking back up at the mirror, she smiled to test the look. Then she noticed a tear slipping down her cheek as the smile slipped away from her lips. There was a stranger looking back at her in the mirror.

When she walked back out into the room, the conversation stopped. Mitchell, the blond man, looked mad.

Sandi, his fiancée, stood by his side, holding his hand. Sandi's dark skin, hair, and eyes were the complete opposite of her fiancé's.

Carter, the chocolate-eyed man, had his arms crossed over his chest and a stern look on his face.

She started to take a step back towards the restroom, but then Mitchell spoke. "Carter and Sandi think that it's best to hide you away from the world for a while. Carter wants to take you up to his place in Maine. I think that you need to face this situation head-on, no pun intended. I think you need to come back to Manhattan and get right back in the swing of things. Maybe the repetition will jog your memory."

Manhattan? Was she from Manhattan? She took a step back now and came up against the wall.

"See," Carter motioned with his arm, swinging it towards her. "Just the thought of going back to the city scares her. She needs some peace and quiet. She needs some time to recover. What better place to do that than in Rockport? Besides, she's due for a vacation and so am I." Carter looked at her and for a second, she thought there was something else he wasn't saying. She didn't know how she knew it, but at that moment, she knew he had a secret that he wasn't telling his friends. Or her.

The next morning, Eve was wheeled out in a wheelchair from the hospital room with Carter, Mitch, and Sandi trailing behind. When they made it to the lobby, Carter ran out in the snow to pull a car forward. It was a silver sedan and Mitch explained that they'd gathered her luggage from the hotel room. They had talked and made a decision and it was decided that Carter was going to drive her to Rockport, Maine, where they, Carter and her, were going to stay until she felt comfortable returning to New York.

Mitch and Sandi hugged her before she got into the car and assured her they would see her soon. She felt like a lamb being taken to slaughter. Based on the words of what were now strangers to her, she got in the car with Carter and let him drive her away from the only security she could remember.

The clothes she'd dressed in, given to her by Sandi, felt foreign. They fit perfectly and were very nice, but she couldn't remember buying them, or even if they were her style.

The brown leggings with the large burgundy sweater were very comfortable. Even the black boots with the warm insoles were very nice, but she just couldn't stop thinking about how strange everything felt.

She looked down at her arm in the sling and tried to move it a little. Pain shot up her wrist and arm, causing her to hold her breath. Carter looked over at her and she tried to smile, showing him nothing was wrong. There was a frown on his face and a small crease between his brows. Then he turned and looked at the road again and continued his conversation. She watched the snow fall as Carter drove out of the city. He talked almost non-stop and she let him. She'd ask him a few questions here and there, but nothing about her life, just about the scenes that went by as he drove.

Her head still hurt too much to try and remember details and her eyesight was going in and out. At times she could clearly see the houses and barns that they were passing, but at other times, she couldn't even make out the windshield wipers as they cleared the snow from in front of her.

The warmth of the car and the sound of the engine was making her sleepy and her head drooped. She must have slept for a while because when she woke, her neck was twisted and sore from having been stuck in the odd position of leaning against the window.

"How about some lunch?" Carter smiled and handed her a bag from a fast food chain she did remember. "It's one of your favorite sins." He winked at her.

She looked down and opened the bag and pulled out a large hamburger. When she sank her teeth into the juicy burger, she closed her eyes and felt comfort flooding her mouth. It was almost like she hadn't eaten in a year.

"You don't eat these as often as you used to, but I think you can make an exception this time." He had a funny smile on his face and she wondered why he was watching her closely as she ate the rest of her burger.

He pulled back onto the highway and continued to talk to her as they drove. She found his voice soothing and half listened to him talking about his grandparents' place. Before she knew it, she was asleep again, this time with her head resting on the headrest.

It was dark when they pulled into a hotel. Carter ran in the office and dealt with getting them a room. Then he carried their suitcases into their joint room and helped her walk in. When he followed her into the room, she turned and looked at him.

"I'm not leaving you alone. There are two beds." She saw the determination in his eyes and something told her not to argue with him. She was in too much pain at this time, anyway. Her head was throbbing, and her vision had yet to return, so she could only make out shapes beyond two feet away.

"You fell asleep before you could take your pain pill after lunch." He walked to a bag and pulled out a white paper bag. Taking a bottle from it, he handed her two pills and then walked over and filled up a glass of water in the bathroom sink. "Here, you should feel better in an hour or two."

She'd yet to say anything to him since arriving; instead, she downed the pills and walked slowly to the farthest bed and sat on the edge.

"Your suitcase is there if you want to shower and change." He nodded to a large black bag.

Her things were inside it. What would she find? What kind of things did she have? She scooted over and unzipped the bag, looking inside. There were three pairs of shoes: two sets of heels and one pair of running shoes. Sweatpants sat on the top. She grabbed them with her good arm along with a white t-shirt, then went to the bathroom.

Closing the door, her head spun as she leaned against the cold door. She was having a difficult time keeping her eyes open as she showered and dressed. She refrained from using her bad arm as much as she could. Dark bruises ran up her wrist to her elbow. She'd forgotten to grab a comb and as she walked out of the bathroom, she tried to finger comb her hair.

"Here," he handed her a large purple comb. "I thought you might need this." He smiled at her as she sat on the edge of her bed combing her hair. He had the television on to the news. The sound was low enough that it didn't bother her head. "I ordered us some food." He nodded towards a cart. "I'll just go take a shower." He disappeared into the bathroom.

She was too tired to walk over to the cart and see what he'd ordered. Instead, she pulled the covers from her bed and crawled under the cool sheets.

Carter walked out of the bathroom and saw Eve fast asleep. He pulled the blanket up over her shoulder. She was still so pale and there were dark circles under her eyes. The bruise had traveled down her forehead to her cheek. She even had a slight black eye. She still wore the dark sling for her arm and had it tucked close to her body.

Gently, he brushed a strand of her wet hair away from her forehead and looked at her stitches. She'd taken off the bandages. He knew they needed replacing but didn't think it would hurt to keep them off for one night. The cut was looking better. No signs of infection, which Laura had warned him about.

He walked over to the cart and frowned when he saw that she hadn't touched her food. She'd only taken three bites of her burger at lunch before she'd fallen asleep again. He'd been warned that her appetite might not return for a few days.

She was already on the thinner side of his liking, and he didn't think she could stand to lose any more weight. He'd just have to force her to eat a big breakfast tomorrow.

He sat on the edge of his bed and watched her for a while. He'd thought about a lot of things during the long drive while she'd slept. He had a list of things he knew needed to be done to his grandparents' place and a list of people he needed to contact so he could cancel his meetings for the next month. There was so much he'd have to do when they made it to Rockport, including trying to track down her mother.

He leaned his head back and listened to the news while watching her sleep in the bed beside him.

The next morning, they stopped at a little diner and he ordered her a large breakfast full of her favorite foods.

She sat across from him, almost in a zombie state. She said very little and usually only nodded when he asked her questions. Again, she only nibbled on her food and when he mentioned that she could only take her medicine on a full stomach, she ate her toast and drank her orange juice.

"It will have to do for now, but you'll need to eat more for lunch." She nodded and looked away. She'd found a pair of large sunglasses in her bag that covered most of the bruising. Her hair had been pulled back with the exception of a few strands that helped hide the scar and coloring of her forehead.

When they drove away from the diner, she rested her head against the window and was fast asleep within minutes. She woke shortly before lunch and ate a little more than she had for breakfast. After they were on the road again, she swallowed her pain pills and tried to stretch out next to him in the seat. He'd pulled out one of his sweatshirts for her to roll up and use as a pillow against the window. She snuggled with it like it was the most comfortable thing she'd ever had.

He didn't know how she could sleep that long, but then remembered that the nurse had told him the pain pills would make her groggy. He'd see if she felt like she could cut back to only one pill next time.

When the countryside started looking familiar to him, he felt excitement rushing through him. He'd be glad to get out of the car and be home. They drove through Rockport just after dusk, the small town had never looked better.

He noticed a few changes to Main Street. There were a few new shops and a few that had closed down. He'd called ahead to his neighbor, Mr. Johnson, and had him stock the place with food and firewood. The old man had been a dear friend to his grandparents and had been keeping an eye on the place since their deaths.

Carter sent him a check each year to cover any expenses and a little something extra for his trouble. The old man always sent the check back to him with a kind note saying he didn't need anything and he was just helping out a neighbor.

As he drove up with Eve still asleep next to him, the headlights cut the fog and he saw the huge gray place for the first time in almost four years. His grandfather had built this place for his family when Carter's mother had been just a child. The white trim and bright red door were in need of some fresh paint.

From what he could see, the trees and bushes surrounding the place were still neatly trimmed, no doubt thanks to Mr. Johnson. The snow hadn't let up and when he thought of the cold in the house, he shivered. Parking the car by the front porch, he left it running and rushed in to turn on the heat and start a fire to warm the place.

When he entered the house, he was happily surprised to feel heat hit his face. There on the banister was a note from Mr. Johnson.

"Thought you might get in sometime tonight. I turned the heat on and left a pile of firewood inside for you. The

pantry is stocked. Your luggage from New York arrived earlier. Eve's bags are in your grandparents' room. Yours are down the hall. I'll stop by tomorrow and check in on you both. --L. Johnson."

They just don't make neighbors like that in New York, Carter thought, and he shook his head as he set the note back down. When he walked back out to the front porch, he could see Eve awake in the car, looking out of the window and staring at the house. Did she remember this place? Would being here jog any memories?

He looked at her through the glass and couldn't see any recognition in her eyes. Instead, she looked tired and cold.

Rushing to the car, he helped her out. "Go ahead inside, I'll grab the bags."

She took a few steps and stood under the large overhang on the front porch and turned to wait for him as he grabbed the two bags from the trunk. When he stopped in front of her, he realized she'd put on his sweatshirt and had her good hand tucked into the large pockets, while the one in the sling was tucked somewhere under the large sweatshirt. The thing hung down halfway to her knees and looked very sexy on her with just her black leggings and boots underneath.

"This is your grandparents' place?" She looked at him and he thought for a second that he could see the old spark in her eyes.

He nodded, not wanting to say anything and break the spell. He wanted to step closer to her, gather her up and never let her go, but instead, he walked past her into the warmth of the house.

"Mr. Johnson stopped by earlier and turned on the furnace for us. Sandi and Mitch sent that luggage we talked about. I know you don't like people going through your things, but I didn't think the three pairs of shoes you had packed would keep you satisfied for too long." He turned towards her with a grin on his face. He was awarded with a smile from her.

"Was I that vain?" She stood just inside the door, looking around.

He laughed and set the bags down. "If I say yes, will you hit me?" He couldn't help teasing her; after all, he was home. She was here, healthy and alive, and they were together. He felt energy rushing through his veins. Somehow, the old place always did that to him. Especially when she was here with him.

"You're looking more refreshed." He walked over and flipped on a few lights. He saw her shiver. "I can start a fire down here if you want."

"No, it's okay." She turned and looked in towards the living room.

"Are you hungry?" He felt a wave of awkwardness hit him and for a split second and felt like a teenager on his first date again.

"No." She walked into the entryway and stopped in front of a table that held a silver frame with an old photo in it.

"Is this your family?" She picked the frame up and looked at it.

He walked over beside her and looked at the picture, frowning. There in bold colors were Mitch, Carter, and Eve sitting on the summer beach a few yards from where they stood. Their childish smiles made it very obvious that they'd just spent the day water skiing and playing in the surf. He didn't remember the exact day or what they had done after, just that it had been another wonderful day with his best friends. No doubt, they were getting ready to have a large bonfire on the beach and cook hot dogs and marshmallows over the flame while listening to his grandfather's spooky stories as his grandmother pretended to be scared. He frowned even more and thought of what he had truly lost in the back alley in Chicago. "Yes, that's my family."

CHAPTER 5

It took her a while to get settled in. Eve, she kept telling herself to think of herself as Eve. Even though the name was strange, she played it over and over in her head. Looking around the house, she wondered what she was doing here, in Rockport, Maine, with Carter, a complete stranger. She thought about it, and actually, everyone was a complete stranger to her, now. From all that she'd overheard in the hospital, Carter was her business partner, along with Mitchell. Apparently, the three of them had been best friends since childhood.

She sat on an overly large couch that was more comfortable than it looked, as Carter busied himself with cleaning the house. They'd arrived two days ago, but she had spent most of it asleep or lying in the large bed with the biggest headaches in the history of humans. When he came down with an armful of linens, he smiled at her.

"Sorry, it's been a while since I've been here. Mitch and Sandi stayed here last year, but I just haven't had time to visit and clean up the place." He dumped the items on the floor and walked over to sit beside her. "Are you doing okay? You sure did sleep awhile."

"Yes, the pain has been cut in half." She still felt pressure on her head but didn't want to spend any more time upstairs in the large room, alone.

"Do you need another pain pill?" He started to get up.

"No." She reached out and stopped him from moving. "I'm fine. Really."

"Okay." He frowned a little. "If you feel like you need one, just let me know."

She nodded and looked down at the photo album he'd given her. There were hundreds of pictures of the three of them, Mitch, Carter, and herself. Younger images, older ones. It seemed they were always together. She felt a little better knowing there was proof behind what Mitchell and Carter had told the hospital. They had been best friends since grade school.

"Where are my parents?" In all the pictures she'd seen, none had shown anyone whom she thought could be her mother or father. There had been an older couple, but underneath the picture, it had said, "Mary and Steven Edwards." She knew they must be Carter's grandparents.

"Well," he said and played with a strand of her hair. She flinched a little, and he pulled his hand away, looking down at his fingers with a slight frown. "Well, your parents live just outside of New York. I've been told your dad is out of the country at the moment." He stood up and picked up the pile of dirty linen. "I'll just go throw these in the washer. Why don't you head up and rest a while? I'll make us some soup then you can take another pain pill." He turned to leave, then looked back at her. "I'll keep trying to get a hold of your folks, don't worry." He walked out, down a long hallway.

After he was gone, she slowly stood up. She still felt waves of dizziness hit her, but it was getting better. Taking the picture book with her, she made her way to the twisted staircase that sat in the middle of the house. She stood at the bottom and looked all the way up the three floors to a large chandelier that hung over the opening. By the time she got to the top of the stairs, she was a little breathless. She walked down a long hallway. Here there were framed pictures of some of the better shots she'd seen in the photo album. Her face, the one that she'd seen for the first time just three days ago, smiled back at her in most of the images, almost always next to Mitchell or Carter.

She opened the door to the master suite and looked in. She hadn't really noticed it before; her head had hurt too much. Now as she looked around she noticed that the room was large with a very big four-poster bed that sat off to one side. A huge television sat on a stand across from the bed. She set the photo book down next to it and walked into an adjoining room, which was a newly remodeled bathroom. When she walked in, she smiled at the huge bathtub. She'd taken a quick shower at the hotel on their drive to Maine but hadn't bothered to shower since. She was looking forward to taking a long, hot bath.

When she looked across the room at the mirror, she was still shocked to see her reflection. It was hard to explain; it was like looking at a stranger who followed your every movement. The first time she'd seen herself, she'd felt a sense of relief. Not that she was vain—at least she didn't think she was—but she'd been happy that she was pretty. Very pretty.

Her dark hair had been matted with dried blood. It had been caked on her forehead as well. It had taken her almost fifteen minutes to slowly clean it off her sensitive skin. She'd actually left most of it in her hair, since trying to clean it had given her a larger headache and her vision had grayed at times. The last thing she wanted to do was faint in the shower and have someone come in and find her like that.

Walking closer to the mirror, she assessed herself now. The new white bandage was over her cut, which had apparently received half a dozen stitches. Her left arm was still in a sling and when she tried to move it, she found out why it was better to keep it on and still.

There were still a lot of questions she had about her relationships with everyone, especially her relationship with Carter, but she didn't quite know how to ask. She hadn't wanted to ask Sandi or Mitchell, so she had decided to wait and feel it out.

Walking back over to the tub, she started filling it with hot water. When she leaned over to plug it, she saw that there were jets in the tub. She was going to really enjoy this. She hit the button to turn on the jets and they made a crazy sound and a little water sputtered out. Quickly, she turned it off again. She knew that once the tub was full, the jets would help soothe all he aches she had.

She moved over to the bathroom door and closed it, hitting the lock button. She might not know what her relationship with Carter was, but she didn't think a private bath would cause any problems.

Slowly, she removed her clothes and her bandages. She left the small white butterfly bandages over her stitches but removed everything else. She'd been too foggy to really get a good look at her body when she'd dressed. Her eyesight had recovered a little more now and she stood in front of the mirror assessing herself. She started to slowly turn and was shocked to find a small tattoo which started at her lower right rib and went down to her upper hip. She couldn't tell what it said, and at first, she thought it was in a different language. But then she realized it was the mirror image and calculated in her mind, reversing the words until finally, she realized it said, *"To thine own self be true"* in small fancy cursive letters. She laughed.

"If only I could." She finished her assessment of her body and walked over to sink into the warm water. She hit the button for the jets and felt the sore muscles in her back start to relax. The doctors and nurses had told her to try and not push herself to remember, that it would come eventually.

But she just couldn't shut down her mind. At this point she had images, but none of them flashed in her head as memories. The only steady thing so far was the sound of Carter's voice. When she heard him speak, she felt something. She wasn't sure what it was, but the first word that popped into her head was safety.

She leaned back in the tub and when her hair floated around her, she reached up and tried to scrub the rest of the dried blood from her hair. She noticed a small patch near her injury that had been cut really close to her scalp. It was small enough that she figured she could easily part her hair on the other side for a while until it grew back.

She sat up a little and grabbed the shampoo, using it to get the rest of the blood. Finally, minutes later, she felt she had sufficiently removed all of the caked-on blood from her skin and scalp. Her head hurt a little from the tugging and pulling she'd done to get it all. Resting back, she rinsed her hair and relaxed with the jets.

Her mind kept flashing back to the hospital room. What secret did Carter have that he didn't want his friends to know? She'd heard the story of how she'd been injured, at least the part when Carter had found her in a dark alley, bloody and unconscious.

How had she gotten there? Where had he been? Did he have something to do with how she'd been injured? As soon as that thought crossed her mind, she shook her head no. There was no way Carter would ever hurt her. She may not have her memory back, but she knew, just knew in her heart that that much was true. So many other questions raced through her mind.

Half an hour later, when she opened the bathroom door, she screamed and started to fall backward.

While Carter stood outside the bathroom door waiting for Eve to get out of the bath, he thought that if he was ever going to pick up the habit of biting his nails, he would have done so then. Instead, he had paced back and forth, listening at the door. Did she know how dangerous it was for her to be taking a bath? What if she slipped and hit her head? What if she started to feel light-headed, something he'd noticed she'd done several times in the last two days, even though she never mentioned it.

The minutes had ticked by slowly, and he was just about to barge in when the bathroom door opened, and he jumped as Eve squealed. Then she had started to fall, and he'd reached out and grabbed her. He pulled her close to him, so she wouldn't fall. She felt so warm and soft and smelled so good.

"What do you think you're doing?" she said, just as he said the same.

"What do you think you're doing? Don't you know how dangerous it is for you to be locking yourself in a bathroom, taking a bath?" He held onto her as she was trying to get out of his hold. The large white towel she'd wrapped herself in was slipping a little, and she'd tried to pull it up and push him away at the same time.

"I was in no immediate danger. What were you doing standing outside the door?" She glared at him. He could feel her chest rise and fall with each breath. The skin he was holding on to was wet and warm and he didn't want to let go. She smelled of lilies and it dawned on him that she was all but naked in his arms. He decided he didn't want to let go anytime soon.

"Did you enjoy your bath?" he asked her softly.

She blinked a few times. It was a look he knew well— the look she had right before she was about to scold him for changing subjects.

"Don't." He interrupted her thoughts. "Don't lecture me on changing subjects." When a shocked look crossed her face, he smiled. "You may not know who you are, but make no mistake about it, I do. I know your moods, I know when you're happy when you're sad." He looked down at her lips and smiled when she licked them. His eyes traveled back to hers and he saw them cloud over with desire. "When you want to be kissed." He leaned his head down towards her mouth and placed a soft kiss on her lips. She tasted as good as she felt, and she seemed to melt in his arms. Her hand snaked around his neck and pulled him closer. He moaned as she slid her fingers into his hair.

He couldn't stop his hands from traveling between the soft cotton and her heated skin. How did she make her skin so soft? It felt like silk under his fingertips. Her wet hair had been brushed and lay down her back. He enjoyed the smoothness of it as his hands roamed over her body while their mouths pleasured each other. He wanted her, there was no denying the fact, but when he thought about her, it was her fire that he wanted. He was a schmuck. What was he doing, taking advantage of her like this? Slowly he pulled back and looked down at her closed eyes. Her dark eyelashes rested on her high cheeks. He wanted nothing more than to kiss every inch of her face and her body but now was not the time.

"Carter?" Her eyes were open, and she was looking at him. "What exactly am I to you?"

He knew it took a long time for him to answer her, but a million scenarios played through his mind at that moment. Here was a unique opportunity. They were going to be alone in this house for who knows how long. Mitch was handling the business, so there was no rush to get back to New York. Her parents, well, who knew where they were. He thought of all the fights and arguments they'd had over the years. Eve had never let him get this close before. Sure, there were the two nights before her attack, but he could blame her state of mind on having to get her drunk first. Looking down at her face, he knew she wasn't drunk now.

Then a light went off in his mind. This was his one clean shot at happiness. She might just kill him if she ever got her memory back, but the odds were in his favor that she'd be so in love with him, that it wouldn't matter. He decided that was a chance he was willing to take and opened his heart and told her what he'd been feeling for as long as he could remember.

"Eve, you are everything to me. You're the woman I'm going to marry." He watched her eyes get bigger, then soften and he knew that maybe, just maybe, he had a chance of happiness.

CHAPTER 6

Eve sat across the room and watched him cook in the large kitchen. She enjoyed seeing him move around as he hunted for pans or dishes.

"It's been a while since we've been here." He smiled at her. "I've forgotten where everything is."

He found the plate he'd been hunting for and set it near the stove, then looked at her. "So, you really don't remember anything? Like foods you like or don't like?"

She shook her head. "Why? Is there something in particular that you had in mind?"

He laughed. "No. You pretty much liked it all. We never could tell how you could stay so skinny after eating more than us." He turned back to the fish he had simmering in a pan. "Of course, you're quite the runner. Never could beat me though." He looked back at her and she didn't know how she knew it, but she knew he was lying. Instead of saying so, she just smiled.

"So, tell me something else about myself." She leaned her elbow on the countertop and watched him. He had a

71

nice body. His shoulders were wide, and his hips were narrow. When he bent over to check on the potatoes in the stove, she enjoyed the way his worn jeans looked over his tight backside.

"Well, you're an only child, like Mitchell and myself. We went to Huntington School district our whole lives until we graduated, then we all went to Princeton. It was a big shock when we were all accepted together. Shortly after, Mitch and I started K&E Agency. A few years back…" He trailed off. His back was to her, so she couldn't see his face, but then he picked right back up. "A few years later you came on board and the rest is history."

"Why didn't I start the business with you?" She watched his body movements, waiting for any sign.

"You had received an offer from a larger company. You went and worked there until you decided it wasn't for you anymore." He turned back to her and smiled. "Here, you can set the table." He motioned to the plates and silverware.

She got up and started setting them on the large table. "This was your grandparents' house. From the pictures, it seems I spent a lot of time here."

"Yes," he smiled over at her. "Every summer, you and Mitch would stay, up until we were done with college. Just before my grandparents died."

"How did they die?" She looked over at him.

"My grandmother died of cancer shortly after we graduated college. My grandfather died in his sleep shortly after that. My mom thinks he died of a broken heart."

"Your mother? Where is she?" She sat up a little.

"She died two years ago." He turned back around and tried to busy himself with cooking.

"I'm sorry, Carter." She sat back and thought about it. "Do you still have your father?"

He turned to her and looked into her eyes. "I never really had my father. He left when I was little. Hasn't shown his face since I was three years old." He shrugged his shoulders. "My grandparents and many uncles and aunts, my cousins, all filled in where my family was lacking. Not to mention I had you and Mitch to keep me company."

He leaned against the countertop while the fish sizzled. "My grandfather built the place when all their kids were young. My mom was one of eight. Most of them are gone now since mom was the youngest of the bunch. She lost two brothers in Vietnam, a sister in a fire a few years later, and the rest are off somewhere else with their own families. When my grandparents died, they left the house to my mom and when she died, well, the place came to me." He turned around and took the fish off the stove.

"Am I close to my folks?" She bit her bottom lip, afraid of the answer.

He looked at her, then walked over and took her hand. "Sorry, sweetie. Your father is a strict military type. Your mother…Well, she falls in line with your dad, and to be honest, I can't remember the last time you saw either of them."

Her shoulders dipped a little. "What about Mitch?"

Carter's eyebrows shot up. "Mitch? Well, his mother lives outside of Boston. She plays tennis three times a week, attends all the country club events, and is sure to have someone younger than us in her bed at least once a week. His father lives in California and pretty much lives the same life."

"Is that the reason we bonded so well? The lack of family?" She helped him carry the food to the table.

He nodded. "That and the incident."

She set the plate down and looked at him. "The incident? What incident?"

He smiled. "I think that's a story for a later time. What do you say we eat?"

She shook her head, "No, you don't. You cannot spring something like that on me and get away with not answering." She crossed her good arm over her chest. It didn't give the whole effect since her left arm was in the sling, but he still got the idea. Finally, he sighed and pulled out a chair for her.

"Okay, but let's start eating first. I'm hungry." He nodded towards the chair for her to take a seat. She walked over and sat down, smiling. She tried to be patient as they dished their food up and both started eating. When half his fillet was gone, he finally looked up at her.

"It was back in grade school. Mitch and I were already friends. You were just this little girl with braces and glasses that followed us everywhere. We thought you had a crush on one of us since you wouldn't leave us alone." He took a sip of his beer. "Mitch had heard from Vance Kyle that Rodney Stoller's cousin had found this really cool hang out place under the freeway. Well, when Vance dared Mitch to go there and spray paint his name on the walls, I decided my best friend couldn't be called a chicken. After all, we were at a crucial time in our lives. Girls were starting to look a lot more like fun to us and that meant we had to impress them. And after all, what about spray painting a cool hangout didn't scream chick magnet?"

Eve laughed, the sound almost shocked her, and she

covered her mouth. Carter smiled. "Go ahead, sweetie. You've always had such a wonderful laugh."

She smiled at him.

"Well, we decided that I would pretend to spend the night at his place and he'd tell his folks he was staying at mine. You know, the old switch-a-roo." She nodded. "So, after school that next Friday, we hopped on our bikes and rode like the wind to our hangout, a tree house we'd built a few summers back with Mitchell's dad. When we got there, you were there. We'd told you a million times not to come there, but you never paid attention to us. We said something mean, like, "Girls suck" and you went off crying. Finally, after ditching you, we packed our stuff on our bikes and took off, using the map Rodney's cousin had made for us. What we didn't know was that in order to get to this cool hangout, we had to cross a busy highway. It took us two hours to find a bridge and cross under. By that time, it was almost dark. Mitch was complaining about it, but I reminded him we had our flashlights and reflectors on our bikes. No ten-year-old thinks he's vulnerable. When we got there, we realized there were a bunch of drunks living under the bridge. They had their barrels full of trash they were burning, and little makeshift homes made out of cardboard boxes. It took us ten minutes of arguing before we finally decided it wasn't worth risking. We tagged both our names on the cement pillar just outside the underpass and started heading back home. But when we got a few yards away, we noticed a pink Barbie bike hidden in the bushes." He shook his head. "So we turned back around and rushed back to the bridge, thinking the worst." He picked up his beer and took a slow sip. Then he picked up his fork and started eating again.

"Well?" She leaned closer. "What happened next? What was the incident?"

He looked across from her, his eyebrows raised. "What do you think happened?"

She thought about it, tried really hard to pull any sliver of memory from her brain. Nothing. She shook her head and noticed his eyes dull a little as he frowned.

"When we got to the bridge, we looked on from the bushes, too afraid to go out in the open with so many scary people. Finally, as we were about to turn back and go for help, we heard you laugh. Slowly, we stepped out from our hiding spot and followed the sound. We found you sitting next to an old woman, holding a cat that looked like it had been run over ten times. There were a few other people sitting around the fire with you and you were telling them all about your two best friends, Mitchell and Carter."

"I wasn't afraid of them?" She couldn't see or imagine her ten-year-old self doing something so brave.

He shook his head. "No, not only were you not afraid of them, you ended up going back there once a month for two years to talk to that old woman. We tagged along, just to make sure you were safe."

"Of course, you did." She smiled at him. "What happened?"

His smile faltered. "They found her, the old woman, one winter, frozen to death. Someone had stolen her blankets and boots."

Eve's eyes turned damp and she realized she was crying for a woman she didn't remember. "Why?"

"Why did they steal her stuff? Probably to keep warm themselves."

"No, why did I go back every month? Why would I do

such a thing? Why would you let me do something so dangerous?" She stood and carried her dishes to the kitchen, hating the tears that were streaming down her face. She set her dish in the sink, half-eaten food and all. Leaning on the counter, she frantically wiped at the tears.

"Sweetie, there was no stopping you." He stood right behind her. Then his hands went to her shoulders and he turned her around to face him. His fingers reached up and wiped her tears away gently. "When you got something into your head, there was no stopping you. You had shown up two ten-year-olds who thought they were the bravest of the brave. You, a ten-year-old, Barbie-bike-riding girl. You were much stronger and braver, we just had to be your friends. From that night on, the three of us were inseparable."

He pulled her close, her face buried in his shoulder. "I'm sorry. I don't know why I'm crying over someone I don't even remember."

"Eve," he pulled back and looked down at her. "Stella was like a grandmother to you. You'd never had a grandmother before. That summer, after she died, your folks let you come up to my grandparents' house. You and my grandmother instantly hit it off and were always together from then on. Just look at the pictures all over the house. You were the granddaughter she never had. I have a lot of cousins, boys, all of them." He smiled and pulled her close again.

She went to bed in the large soft bed that night and her mind refused to shut down. She wished for images to pop into her head, memories of the events Carter had described, but nothing did. She picked up the photo book and started looking through it again.

There were so many pictures of the three of them together, but none of the images showed any clue that she and Carter were an item. When had they become an item? Was it recently? What had sparked that first interest from friendship to something else?

She had so many other questions but didn't quite know how to ask him. It would have been a lot easier if she'd had a few close girlfriends she could ask.

Looking at the pictures, she realized there wasn't even a picture of her with any girlfriends. Did she have any close ones?

She set the book back down and tried to close her eyes, but images kept flashing under her dark eyelashes. Getting up, she walked over and flipped on the television. Watching the news, she finally fell asleep.

CHAPTER 7

$\mathcal{C}$arter watched the sunrise from the beach. Winter was just around the corner. Since he was going to be around the old place for a while, he might as well get some of the work done that was needed. Yesterday, while Eve had napped, he'd called someone to see about re-roofing the huge place. There were only a few shingles that needed fixing, but he decided to replace the whole thing instead. It had been about fifteen years since it had been replaced. The electric and plumbing were all good to go, and since the furnace had been pumping out heat since they had arrived, all seemed to be working fine.

He had plans to paint several of the rooms, and although he knew his grandmother loved the flower wallpaper in the dining room, he had plans to replace it. Not to mention that the furniture could use an update as well. Although the mauve-flowered couch was an eyesore, it still was the most comfortable couch he'd ever sat on. Maybe he could have it reupholstered. The grand piano still sat in the window alcove and was in mint condition.

As his grandfather's prized possession, none of the kids were allowed to play with it without him on hand. It could probably use a tuning and a good dusting, but he bet the thing still played like new.

There were a couple of loose floorboards here and there and the light in one of the closets needed repair. Since the place had six bedrooms and five bathrooms, he knew there were a lot of other things that would need to be done.

When he started walking back towards the house, he spotted Eve walking towards him. Her long strides ate up the beach, so he met her halfway.

"Morning." He noticed she'd worn a pair of his old sweats that he'd probably left in one of the drawers somewhere. She also had on one of his old Princeton sweatshirts on. Her hair was tied back in a long ponytail and her cheeks were a little pink. "Out for a morning walk?"

"Yes." She looked around and smiled. "It's so peaceful here. Is it always like this?"

He laughed. "Yeah, pretty much. The only time I can remember it being crowded was when we had parties." He looked around too. The beach was deserted, and he knew it would remain so most of the winter. The nearest neighbor was a way down the road and he was in his late seventies. "When we were in college, staying up here for the summers, we had a lot of parties." He smiled and took her hand and started walking back towards the house. He knew she was feeling better, but he didn't think that too much cool air would do her any good. She needed rest and to stay off her feet. At least that's what the doctor had said.

"Yeah, I saw a few pictures. Maybe you can sit down with me and tell me who everyone is. At least the people

I'll need to know for future reference." She was gazing off towards the sound.

"Is that a lighthouse?" She pointed to the rocky cliff and an old building.

"Yeah, we can take a walk there some day. What do you say to some hot chocolate and French toast? I have the roofing guys coming in about an hour, but I can squeeze in making us some breakfast."

"Hmmm, sounds good." He enjoyed the feel of her small hand in his and he could tell she was in deep thought as they walked back towards the house.

When they hit the clearing, he glanced around the place. The yard would need some work next spring, but so far, the company he'd hired the last few summers had done a great job keeping it up. He knew the pool had been drained and had sat empty since the first summer he'd owned the place.

The yard could stand for a few flowers, though. His grandmother had always had flowers everywhere. He looked off towards her rose garden and sighed when he saw the state the bushes were in. Just then Eve stopped. He looked over at her and her eyes were huge.

"What? What is it? Are you dizzy?" He reached for her and held her close.

"I…I think I remember your grandmother. I just had a flash." She reached up and touched her forehead. "There was a woman in a large hat with a blue bow on it. She was bending over, digging in the dirt with a red spade."

He smiled and kissed her forehead. "Yes!" He leaned back and looked into her eyes. "That was our grandmother." He noticed a tear on her cheek and wiped it away gently. "You two would disappear into the garden for hours."

"I had my first memory." She smiled up at him. "What a wonderful memory." Then she put her hand to her head and frowned. "Ohh." She held onto his arm and he saw her face go pale.

"What?" He held her tighter.

"I'm dizzy." He could see her eyes become unfocused. Swooping her up quickly, he rushed into the house with her in his arms. Setting her on the couch, he sat beside her. "Do you want some water? What about an aspirin?"

"No, I'm fine now. I think I'll just rest a while." She leaned back on the cushions. "You said something about French toast and hot cocoa?"

He smiled and stood up. "Stay put. Hot food coming up." He rushed out and into the kitchen. Less than half an hour later, he walked in with a tray full of food. When he walked in, she was asleep, the large comforter his grandmother had made covering her almost completely. He set the tray down and sat next to her, watching her sleep until the roofers drove up outside.

When he came back inside after getting the men started, Eve was sitting up finishing the plate of food he'd left for her.

"Sorry if it was cold. You were resting when I bought it in." He sat beside her and propped his feet on the coffee table.

"That's okay. It was still warm." She drank the rest of her hot chocolate. "Thank you, it was delicious." She leaned back and put her feet next to his, crossing them at the ankles. "You're fixing the place up?" She nodded towards the men outside the large picture window. There was half a dozen of them, scurrying about trying to get ladders and other equipment ready.

"Yeah, I can pretty much do everything else myself. But, well, you know how I feel about heights." He leaned his head back and closed his eyes.

She chuckled. "No, I don't. But I guess I can piece together that you're not too fond of them." She watched his eyes open and a hint of sadness crossed his face.

"Oh, yeah. I guess I forgot." He closed his eyes again.

"What else are you going to be doing around here?" She looked around the large room, trying to imagine what it could look like. The furniture in the room was old and very much out of date, but the room was solid and had great potential. With a fresh coat of paint, new curtains, new furniture, the room would be more up to date. She could just imagine how rearranging the furniture would open the room up and make it flow better.

"Was I any good at decorating?" She tilted her head, trying to remember.

"Hmmm, yes. You helped Mitch redecorate his place after the Suzanne incident."

"Now you've got me curious. What was the Suzanne incident?" She watched the men working outside and listened to Carter tell her all about yet another part of her past that she no longer remembered.

That evening she decided to try and cook something. Since they'd been there, Carter had been the only one moving around the kitchen. She'd been curious if she could cook. A few minutes later, she had her answer.

The fire alarm was blaring as Carter ran in, sheer panic on his face. He'd been cleaning out his grandfather's old office, and there was dust all over his shirt and pants. Eve tried not to laugh, but the scene was almost too much. The pan she'd used had black things floating in the oil.

Carter rushed over and put the lid on the pan, sufficiently snuffing out the blaze that had been building. "What are you doing? You know damn well you're not allowed to use this kitchen. Not after the cake incident." He carried the pan to the sink and turned on the water. As a large pile of steam rose and almost hit him in the face, she crossed her arm and raised her chin.

"No, I don't know. I don't remember! I don't know anything about what I can and can't do. I can't remember anything about being here before. About you!" She stomped her foot as he turned towards her. "I don't know if I can cook. I don't know if I know how to drive a car, or what my favorite book is. I don't remember my first kiss or my mother's name. I don't know if I like chocolate or vanilla." She walked towards him and shoved her finger into his chest. "I don't remember you or even if I still liked you. I can't remember why we were in Chicago or what happened to me that night. I don't even know how I got this bump on my head. So far, all you want to tell me about are the good, 'safe' things like your grandparents." She air quoted around the word safe. She threw her hand up in the air and raised her chin a little more. "I don't even know why I feel a very strong urge to kiss you and to throttle you at the same time." She turned and stormed out of the room and made it all the way upstairs before he spun her around.

"Wait just a minute. I'm sorry, I forgot." She could see the sadness in his eyes again, and it tore at her a little more. "I'll answer any questions you have." He rubbed his hand over his forehead and she could tell he was tired. He walked over and sat in the soft chair under the window, closing his eyes and resting his head on the back.

"Do you need some help?" She watched his eyes fly open.

"Help? In the office? No." He shook his head.

"Listen. Since it's obvious that I'm no good in the kitchen and you've confirmed that I am good at decorating, maybe I can give you a hand."

He shook his head again. "No. You're not supposed to overdo it." He stood up and started to walk out. "Your arm is still in a sling and just this morning you almost passed out when walking." He stopped and looked over at her. "Were you hungry? Is that why you were in the kitchen?"

She shook her head. "I was just seeing if I could cook. I wanted to make you dinner since you were working so hard."

He smiled. "Well, now you know. Avoid cooking, cats"—he ticked things off with his fingers as he talked—"riding a unicycle while juggling, oh, and most impor-tantly…staplers." He smiled and walked out.

She blinked. "Staplers? Why staplers?" She rushed after him as he laughed.

Carter knew that Eve was getting restless. He could see that look she got in her eyes when she was bored. And she was very bored a few days later. She'd taken her arm out of the sling and swore to him that it was feeling better, but he could see that she kept it close to her and didn't use it when lifting things. But he agreed that she could help him sort through all his grandparents' stuff. He had a large storage unit delivered the day after the roofers had finished the roof. The metal box sat on the drive and was already half full of items he planned on selling. Already he was thinking he'd need at least two more storage devices just to hold everything.

There were boxes and boxes of paperwork that Eve was going through. She was shredding the unimportant items and placing paperwork that he would want to keep in a large box. She'd found his grandparents' wedding license, copies of all his aunts' and uncles' birth certificates, as well as his own.

"My grandfather was very cautious. He always kept

copies of important documents. After he died, I found a stack of the same stuff in a deposit box at the bank." He chuckled and got back to his job. He'd carried every piece of furniture out of all the rooms downstairs.

Eve had called around and found a local place that would reupholster the couch and two chairs in the living room. They'd picked out the new material from the patches the woman had brought with her. He'd smiled when the older woman had assumed that he and Eve were newly-weds. Then when she'd found out that it had been his grandparents' place, she'd gone on and on about them like they'd been best friends.

The moving van had come and hauled the three large pieces away to her store the next day. Everything else downstairs was being sold, except the piano, the dining room table and chairs, and his grandfather's desk.

"Where are you going to buy everything, you need to replace all this?" Eve stood around in the now empty main floor of the house, her hands on the hips of an old pair of his worn jeans. The legs were rolled up to just above her ankles. She'd become accustomed to wearing his Princeton sweatshirt and she'd found an old bandana to tie her hair up with. He found the outfit oddly appealing.

"Well, I had planned on ordering some of the stuff. I know there's an old antique store in town. Maybe we can head in and look around someday. I've got to stop by the hardware store and pick up some paint and supplies so I can get started on a few items."

He looked down at his feet and frowned. The hardwood floors his grandfather had installed the year he built the house were in dire need of sanding and staining. Something else to add to his list.

"What?" She looked at her feet.

"Hmm, I've never sanded and stained a floor before." He looked up at her and smiled. "Looks like we'll be learning how to do that together.

That evening after having quick turkey sandwiches, Eve went upstairs to soak in the tub. She'd taken to enjoying the bubbles every night. Carter didn't mind sleeping down the hall in the other room on the top floor. It was a little girlie for his liking since the room used to be his mother's, but he found it comforting looking around and seeing all her things around him.

When he heard the water draining from the tub, he walked into his bathroom and started a shower. He knew the water heater could only accommodate a bath and a short shower before needing more time to heat the water.

He'd tried over the last few days to keep his distance from Eve. Every time he forgot that she'd forgotten everything, it was like opening the wound again. The frustration on her face told him everything he needed to know. She hated not remembering as much as he hated it.

Every day she was trying to push herself more, physically. She wanted to carry larger boxes, work longer hours; she'd even taken up walking with him in the mornings. He wouldn't tell her, but he'd cut his walks by half since she'd started tagging along. Still, it was nice having her along.

They used that time to talk about her past. She'd ask questions and he'd answer, filling in every little detail he could remember. The weather was growing colder, and he was sure that any day now they would see snow. He'd made sure the firewood was stacked up and even spent an hour or two chopping kindling. He thought about having a fire, but then remembered the fireplace probably hadn't been used in a while. He'd better have it checked out first.

After five minutes in the shower, the water started to turn cold and he flipped it off. Maybe while he was at the hardware store tomorrow, he'd look into a new water heater.

He'd just walked out of the bathroom, a towel wrapped around his waist when he heard Eve scream. Racing down the hall, he barged into the room and saw her standing half-naked on a chair. She had a shoe in one hand and was holding her towel in the other.

"What?" He looked around, trying to find what she'd screamed about. "What is it?"

"There!" She pointed to her bed. "It crawled under the bed. It was huge!" She got further up onto the chair and held the shoe close to her.

He walked over to the bed, lifted the blanket and knelt down. It was too dark to see anything.

"What is it?" He looked up at her.

"A spider. A huge spider. It had hair!" She shivered and closed her eyes.

"A spider?" He stood up slowly and dropped the blanket. Then he rolled his eyes. "Oh, yeah. I forgot that you're afraid of spiders." He started laughing and walked over to her. "Sorry, sweetie looks like this one got away from you. I'm sure he was more afraid of you then you were of him." He reached for her, but she recoiled.

"I am *NOT* getting down until you kill that monster." She thrust the shoe in his direction.

He placed his hands on his hips and glared at her. "I'm not hunting for a spider that's probably long gone by now."

"Well, I'm not moving until you do." She tilted her

head and he saw a flash of the old Eve there. He knew that even without her memory, she was going to win this battle. Grabbing the shoe from her, he walked over to the other side of the bed just as the small, hairless arachnid crawled out. Dropping the shoe quickly, he sufficiently squashed the thing. Looking up, he smiled at her. "There. That was easy." He made a show of dusting his hands as he walked towards her. "Now, if you don't mind. I'd hate to see you fall off this thing and bonk your head again. I don't think your brain can take it." He laughed.

She put her hand in his and stepped off the chair, but she must have dislodged the rug that covered the wood floors when she'd jumped up there. Instead of smoothly gliding to the floor, she ended up falling right into his chest, knocking him back a step until he tripped over her other discarded shoe and fell backward himself. They landed on the floor with a thud, him on his back, her facing him on his chest. Their legs were tangled, and his breath had been knocked out of his lungs.

"Oh, did you hit your head?" She reached up and started running her hands along the back of his skull. Any pain he felt quickly disappeared as he realized the position they were in. "You did. Oh, you have a knot at the back here." She continued to feel his head as he looked into her face. Her hair had been brushed away from her face, which was clean, and her skin color had finally returned to its natural olive tone. Her eyes were back to their sparkly self and her lips…When he looked at them, he could just imagine how they felt and tasted. His hands had been on her back and when he moved them, he realized he was touching her bare skin. Looking down, he saw her towel was open at the back. She was still busy feeling his head for more bumps when she realized he wasn't paying attention to his injuries.

"Carter?" She started to sit up a little, then realized her towel was no longer wrapped tightly around her body. "Oh." She lay back down on top of him. Her breasts fit perfectly against his chest. "Carter, shut your eyes. My towel has fallen off."

He smiled and shook his head. "I think mine has fallen away, too. You shut your eyes."

She looked down at him and even though he knew the look, there was no way he was going to let her have her way this time. "I guess we'll just have to lie here then." The hand that was on her back started moving slowly across her soft skin.

"How do you get so soft?" He smiled and sniffed her hair that had fallen in his face. "You smell pretty good, too."

She tried to brace herself by holding her hands on either side of his face. "I just had a bath." She looked around. He could tell she was trying to figure out how to wrap the towel around her without exposing herself further. "Just close your eyes for a second." She looked down at him and tried to blow her wet hair out of her face.

He shook his head. "I don't think so. Besides, I like it where I am." He leaned up and started nibbling on her neck, just below her ear. She stopped moving and he thought he heard her moan. Her head dropped a little, giving him more access to her skin, which he took advantage of.

"Carter, I don't think…" She trailed off when his hands started roaming over her back. He felt her arch towards his hands and then her lips were on his as her hands went into his hair and he knew at that moment that all thoughts had left her.

She couldn't explain it if she had to, but he felt right. When his hands roamed over her naked skin, she moaned and wished he would touch her more. She felt herself vibrating as she ran her hands over his chest and arms. They were full of impressive muscles and she wanted to take in everything. He moved a little so that his leg was between hers and she started to move so that her silky skin touched his hairy leg. It felt too good to stop and soon his hands were on her hips as she glided her slick skin over his leg.

"Yes," he moaned against her lips. "Don't stop, don't ever stop, Eve." She couldn't if she wanted to. She was building to something she'd forgotten about. His hands reached up and pulled the cotton away from their skin so they laid there with nothing between them now, heat to heat, and she felt her skin tingle as it met his. She ached and needed him to fill her, to touch her.

His head dipped and when his mouth covered her breast, she jumped at the contact, grabbing hold of his head to keep him close to her. He lapped at her exposed skin and she closed her eyes, tilting her head back to allow him full access.

He moved just a little again and he now he was sitting up, his back against the bed frame, as she was tucked in his lap. She felt his desire next to her heated skin and wanted more than anything to slide onto him and never stop. But he held her hips still as he lapped at her breasts slowly.

"Mmm, let me take my time. We have all the time,

Eve. I want to enjoy every inch of you." His mouth moved to her other nipple as he sucked and licked his way across her heated skin. Her hips kept moving on their own, grinding his hips as her hands held his head to her. She was feeling dizzy and breathless and wanted speed.

"Please, Carter, I can't…"

He stood in one quick motion, carrying her to the bed, and he gently moved over her as he laid her down. "No, this is one place I get to be in control." He smiled down at her. She didn't know what he meant by that. Then he was kissing her again and she forgot everything as his hands and mouth traveled over her body. He trailed down over her ribs as he licked his way to the spot she'd been burning for him to touch. Finally, when his fingers skimmed over the heated flesh, she almost jumped off the bed.

"Easy," he smiled up at her. "So sensitive?"

She nodded her head and grabbed his hand with hers. Pulling it back to the spot she wanted, he chuckled.

"I'm in charge, remember?" He moved her hand away and continued to trail his hand where he pleased. It took a while, but finally, he moved back to the spot she wanted, and his fingers found her wet. She closed her eyes and enjoyed the rhythm he'd found as he moved over her, giving her everything she'd wanted.

He was building her up so fast that when his head dipped, and his mouth touched her skin, she exploded with a scream. Lights flashed behind her eyes and a sharp pain exploded behind her left ear. Together the mixture was almost intoxicating, the pain with the pleasure. Was it always like this?

"More." Carter was leaning over her now. When she looked into his eyes, she saw desire, raw and pure, in them. "I want it all," he growled as he pushed her legs aside, settling between them as he kissed her neck and face. Then he pulled back with a jerk.

"Hang on." He leaned over and yanked open the nightstand drawer, searching. He smiled when he pulled out a small box and shook it. "Whew." They must have been left over from when Mitch and Sandi had stayed there last year.

She frowned as she looked at it, trying to figure out what it was. Then she realized, and she couldn't help but blush. She was happy when she realized he was too busy to notice her heated face. Then he was kissing her again and all embarrassment fled, replaced with want.

When he slid slowly into her, she couldn't stop the moan as he filled her completely. Her legs wrapped around his hips as she held on to his shoulders and hips. Their bodies became slick and the cool sheets on her back clung to her as she moaned with each thrust.

She felt herself building again and wanted more than anything to take him with her this time. When she looked up at him, she noticed his dark eyes on her. He watched her and when she slowly licked her lips and looked at his mouth, his eyes closed, and he swooped down to kiss her as they went together.

It must have been some time before she finally regained her thoughts. Their bodies had cooled, and Carter's body was the only thing keeping her warm from the chill in the house. His breathing had steadied along with hers. She didn't know if he was asleep, but his hot breath on her neck felt nice.

Had she ever felt this way with another man before? He'd said they'd been engaged. How many times had they done this together? Years? Months? Somehow, she didn't think it had been like this before. She wished she could just come out and ask him. But somehow, she thought he'd avoid answering her like he had several times about other subjects she'd brought up.

"Carter?" She rubbed her hands over his backside, enjoying the muscles she found there.

"Mmm?" He buried his face in her hair.

"Where's my engagement ring?" He was causing goose bumps on her skin and she really wished he'd pull the blanket over them or light a fire in the room.

He laughed. "Leave it to you to ask that question at a time like this." He pulled back, resting on his elbows, looking down at her.

She shivered and frowned. "A time like what?"

He shook his head and stood up. "Eve." He walked over and started building a fire. She didn't know how she knew it, but he was struggling with wanting to tell her something.

"What is it, Carter?" He was kneeling down, about to light the fire, but looked over his shoulder at her. "What?" She couldn't see his face in the dark, couldn't see his eyes. "What is it you're not telling me?" She sat up and pulled the blanket over her, trying to warm up.

He turned back to his task. "Nothing. I've told you everything." She looked at his back and knew that his moment of weakness had passed. Would she ever find out what it was he was hiding from her?

CHAPTER 9

Carter watched the flames take hold of the wood. He could feel her eyes bore into his back and knew he'd almost blurted out the truth. How could he have tried to lie to her about them being engaged? It was a moment of weakness. There was no way he was going to spoil the perfect moment that had just happened. In all the years of imagining being with her, nothing had ever compared to the reality of being with her.

Looking over his shoulder, he smiled when he noticed her checking him out. Slowly, he stood and turned. Her eyes traveled over him and he felt himself growing hard again.

Eve's eyes slowly raised to meet his. He smiled and started walking towards her. "The ring is in the downstairs' safe. It was my grandmother's. I haven't had time to come up here and get it for you, yet." He stopped at the side of the bed and pulled the covers away from her. Then he looked down at her and marveled at how beautiful she was. Her knees were up, pushing against her chest and her arms were crossed in front of her. "Shy all of a sudden?" he smiled at her.

She shook her head. "Cold."

"I can fix that." He sat beside her and touched her with his fingertips. Her head fell back, and her eyes slid closed. He could see her relaxing as he ran his fingers over every inch of her. Finally, she was panting when he motioned for her to lie down. She shook her head.

"You got to explore me the first time. I want to see what I've agreed to marry. You lie down. I'll explore and see if something doesn't jog my memory in the process." He almost lost his nerve, but then she smiled at him and he became so turned on, he would have done anything she'd asked of him.

"Lie down." She pointed to the bed and scooted over to make room. He did what she asked, putting his arms behind his head as he leaned back on the pillows.

She sat next to him and ran her eyes over his naked body. "Hmmm." She tilted her head as if she was deep in thought.

He laughed. "What?"

"Nothing pulls at my memory yet." She smiled.

"Maybe if you use one of your other senses," he hinted.

Her eyebrows shot up in question.

"You know… sound, sight, touch, taste…"

"Yes, maybe." She leaned over and started running her fingers over his chest. It was pure torture to sit still as her cool hands ran up and down his heated skin.

"Do you know how badly I want you right now?" His voice sounded strained. His hips came off the bed as she ran her hands down them, then lower, over his legs, as she avoided the one place he wanted her to touch the most.

"Yes, I think I can see how much you want me." She chuckled.

"Eve, you're killing me here." He moaned as she circled again.

"Hmmm, nothing is bringing up memories." His eyes flew open and he watched as she dipped her head to taste his skin. His hips did jump from the mattress then as her tongue licked him, circling and sucking until he thought his eyes would bulge out of their sockets. Somehow, his hands had ended up in her hair, and when his fingers ran over her scar, he pulled them away quickly, not wanting to hurt her, not wanting to remember what had brought them here.

"Eve?" He watched as she sat up, a smile on her lips, then she reached over and took another condom from the box. When he reached to take it from her, she pushed his hands away, playfully.

"I'm in charge this time, remember?" He watched as she opened the package and slowly rolled it down on him. Did she know that the simple act of protection was almost taking him to the edge?

When she was done, he moved to grab her, but she pulled back and shook her head. "No, I'm still in control. All you can do"—she leaned over, her hair resting on his chest as she whispered— "is lie there and take what I give you."

Closing his eyes, he tried to count or think of something that would steady his heartbeat and the desire that was raging in him. Her hands ran over his body, and soon his mind was focused on one thing only. Her.

He felt the bed dip and looked up as she straddled his hips. Now, it would be now. But instead, she sat on his thighs and rubbed her hands over him, gripping him and using her fingers to pleasure him.

"I wonder how long you can go before you lose control." She smiled.

"You little vixen." He smiled up at her. Her skin was shining in the light of the fire. Her eyes sparkled with mischief and desire. That was when he knew he'd lost his heart. His hands came up and gripped her hips, raising her until she hovered above him. "Take all of me." He groaned as she slid down on him fully. Her head fell back, and she gasped. Her hands went to his chest as she held on. "Ride just move." He moaned as she began to move slowly on him.

He tried to let her set the pace, but his hands on her hips started pushing and pulling until their paces matched. He could see her building and knew that he couldn't last much longer. Leaning up, he took her nipple into his mouth and as he sucked, he joined her in the victory.

The next morning, she joined him on the beach for a jog. He made sure to cut his normal run in half, just in case. He didn't want her to push herself too much, yet. The weather was supposed to take a turn later that afternoon, so he spent a good deal of his morning chopping wood and bringing it up to the house. It almost seemed like they had a normal life there in the old house on the bluff. He could almost forget the lies and the reason they were there. The truth and the thought of it surfaced and hung over him like an anvil waiting to fall.

❄

Eve was sitting on the bar stool in the kitchen watching Carter make breakfast when he turned to her, still holding the spatula.

"How about a trip into town today?" He asked.

"Town?" She enjoyed the look of him as he cooked. There was just something sexy about a man in the kitchen.

"Yes." He turned back to expertly flip the spinach and tomato omelet he was making. "There are several antique shops in town and some more along the highway. I thought we'd look for some furniture."

She couldn't explain it, but her heart rate tripled just then. "I must like shopping." She smiled. "My heart is racing, and I think I actually feel dizzy."

He turned and smiled. "Shopping is one of your favorite past times. Mitch and I always hate it when you drag us along."

She laughed.

Four hours later, she was still just as energetic as when they had started shopping five stores earlier. Carter did little complaining, but she knew he was wanting to call it a day. They had picked out several great items for the house including a file cabinet and a bookcase that matched his grandfather's desk in the office.

They were currently at a flea market a few towns away. The large green barn was filled with antique and second-hand items, and she'd lost sight of Carter again. There was quite the crowd in the building that smelled of straw and dust. She chatted with a few people she came across and enjoyed just being out in public. She was looking for some curtains that would go in the living room windows when someone brushed against her side. She felt a wave of dizziness and tried to grip the table in front of her before she hit the floor.

When she opened her eyes again, she was looking into Carter's eyes and knew he was both worried and mad. There were several other people standing around her and she immediately felt embarrassed.

"You have to know your limits. This is all my fault. I should have stopped you an hour ago," Carter said quietly as he pulled her into a sitting position and held up three fingers in front of her.

"Three." She answered his unasked question. "My eyesight is fine." She tried to smile and show him there was nothing to worry about. She wasn't feeling dizzy now. She even felt like her energy levels were still strong. Frowning, she started to get up. "What brought that on? I'm not tired," she asked herself.

"No, don't get up yet." Carter tried to hold her down. "Just wait awhile. Someone is running to get you a bottle of water."

She shook her head. "Carter, I'm fine. I don't feel dizzy. My eyesight is fine, no blurriness. Honestly, besides being a little hungry, I feel fine." She pushed him away until she could stand up. When she did stand, she mentally checked everything as she looked around the barn. Yes, everything was normal. Well, as normal as it could be with a concussion and memory loss.

A short, older woman rushed up to her with a bottle of water. "Here now, drink this down, honey. You'll feel better." She looked towards Carter. "I have an office over there." She pointed towards the side of the barn. "If you want to take her and let her sit for a while. There's a nice sofa for her to lie down for a spell."

Eve shook her head. "No, I'm fine. Really." She drank some of the water and realized she was more than a little hungry. "I suppose I'm just a bit hungry." She smiled. The crowd of people started walking away, leaving her alone with Carter and the older woman.

"There's a wonderful deli just this side of town. You can't miss it. You just let me know if there is anything I can do. I hope you feel better."

"Thank you, I think that was just want she needs," Carter said. The woman walked away, leaving them alone. Carter started pulling her towards the exit.

"Really, Carter. I feel fine. Maybe just some lunch and we can come back. There were these lovely lace valances." She looked over her shoulder as Carter tugged her towards the door.

"Later. Right now, we're going to get you some food and you're going to spend the rest of the day in bed.

An hour later, after stopping by the quaint deli and eating a full turkey sandwich on a toasted wheat roll, she found out he wasn't joking. Every time she tried to get out of bed, he'd said something about calling a doctor. She'd ended up sleeping the rest of the day away. By sunset, she was wide-awake and bored out of her mind. Carter had spent the rest of the day working on his laptop while sitting at the small desk in the room. No doubt he was trying to remain near her so he could watch over her.

That evening after he'd cooked her a large pot of spaghetti, they sat in front of the fireplace and watched an old movie from one of the bookshelves, which was full of old VHS movies. Her feet were tucked underneath her, covered in large wool socks. She looked out the window and noticed snow falling outside.

"Oh! It's snowing." She jumped up and ran to the window to look out. In the porch light, she could see that the large white flakes were sticking to the grass. Carter walked up behind her and wrapped his arms around her, standing behind her as he pulled her close.

"We've had plenty of snowball fights in that yard," he said as he kissed the top of her hair.

"Really?" For just a moment, she closed her eyes and enjoyed the feeling of being held. Had she always felt this way about him? It was hard to explain, but he felt like home, he sounded like home, and he even smelled like home.

"Hmmm, of course, you've never won a battle." He chuckled. "Mitch holds the title of snowball king. There's just something about that guy. You put a ball of snow in his hands and he turned into a maniac."

She smiled as an image of a thirteen-year-old Mitch popped into her head. He was wearing a dark gray jacket that was two sizes too big for his skinny teenage body. His gloves were too small, and he had a dark red knit hat on. He was laughing like a villain from a movie as he threw ball after ball in her direction. Even when she was down on the ground, he stood over her and dumped a handful of snow on her face. Cold seeped into her shirt as snow breached the layers of her protective clothing. Even her feet were wet and cold as the snow penetrated her boots and socks. Mitch stood over her and laughed. "Serves you right. Next time you plan a sneak attack on the King of Snow, you'd better make sure you pack a parka." Mitch stood above her, his hands on his hips as he threw his head back and laughed.

"Eve! Eve?" Someone was screaming at her. The

sound penetrated the memory. She blinked a few times and realized she was lying on the couch, looking up at Carter.

"What?" She tried to sit up. Carter placed his hands on her shoulders, keeping her still. "What happened?"

"You tell me. We were having a nice moment, watching the snow and next thing I know you're taking a face plant, almost through the window."

She looked at his face and realized how pale it was. His hands shook as he held her still and there was pure fear in his eyes. Reaching up, she took his face in her hands.

"I'm sorry, I didn't mean to scare you." Then she remembered what had happened and smiled. "I had a memory." She saw even more fear creep into his eyes and wondered why.

"What?" He pulled back and looked at her. "What memory?"

"A particularly bad snowball fight with the King of Snow." She laughed and then described the scene to Carter as he sat beside her looking troubled. When she was done telling him the memory, he was frowning. "Okay, why are you frowning? From my point of view, it was a great memory. Did something happen?"

"No, it was a fun day. I wasn't there to help you defend yourself because the King had already taken me out and I was stuck under three feet of snow." He chuckled then sobered. "I'm just worried that you're going to pass out every time you remember something. I think we need to go into town tomorrow and have you checked out at the clinic. Maybe even drive into the city and see a specialist." He started to get up, but she grabbed his hand.

"Carter, I'm fine. I don't know why I passed out twice today. Maybe it's my brain's way of trying to heal itself. I feel fine. I don't even have a headache. I'm not dizzy and my vision is fine. Can't we just wait awhile?"

He stood and shook his head. "They told me you might have other symptoms, none of which were passing out every time you remembered something. I think it's best if we have it checked out. Just in case."

For some reason, the thought of going back to a hospital made her feel down like she was taking a step back in her healing. She'd come so far since they'd arrived here. Her arm was almost completely healed, and she'd remembered something. Maybe it was perfectly normal what was happening to her. She started wondering what she had to do to persuade Carter she didn't need to see a doctor.

"Don't give me that look," Carter said from across the room. He was flipping through the phone book, probably trying to find a local doctor.

"What look?" She crossed her arms and glared at him.

"The one that tells me you're about to try and swindle your way out of seeing a doctor." He smiled and went back to flipping through the phone book. Her shoulders slumped a little. It was getting annoying that he had the ability to read her so well.

arter sat out in the waiting room and felt like pacing. The array of beautiful fish that swam happily in a very large tank in the doctor's waiting room did little to calm his nerves. They'd driven into Portland to see a head injury specialist there.

Eve had insisted that he stay in the waiting room while she went back to see the doctor. Since he'd won the two-day battle of coming to the doctor, he considered this a small sacrifice he'd willingly make. Since her first episode, she'd had a total of three fainting spells. Each one lasting longer than the first. It was the one that had happened last night that had finally caused her to agree to come in and be seen. He'd walked in on her in the bedroom, and she'd been lying on the floor, one leg in her pants, one out. She was lucky she hadn't hit her head.

When she'd come to, she'd been so excited that she'd finally had a memory with him in it, even though it had been from when they'd been in high school.

She'd told him about the memory and said she

remembered it like it was yesterday. To be honest, he'd totally forgotten the episode. There had been another teen, Angie something, who had been picking on Eve for ten years. This particular day, Angie, along with a couple of other girls, had placed a large wad of bubble gum on Eve's chair. Then they had followed her around and called her names and pointed it out to everyone.

Eve had shown up at Carter's locker between classes and he'd known something was wrong before she'd made it across the hall towards him. Her face was set in determination and anger.

He smiled now, remembering. There was nothing sexier than seeing Eve angry. Somehow, she just glowed during those times. Maybe that's why in the last few years he'd liked pushing all her buttons.

It took her less than a week to get Angie and the other girls back. But she didn't stoop to their level, no, not his Eve. She went beyond anything that they would have done to her. Instead, she hit Angie where it hurt the most. Angie's boyfriend, Jim, was captain of the football team. He was the type that didn't do a lot of homework but instead chose to spend his time working on his form.

Carter let it slip while talking to a friend in the library —one of the best places to pick up gossip—that he'd seen Jim making out with Angie's best friend Karley. The news took less than three hours to reach the entire school, including Angie. Then they had sat back and watched the whole scene unfold.

Angie and Karley had caused such a scene that the teachers had to separate them. Karley had actually walked away with a large chunk of Angie's hair in her fists. Eve,

Carter, and Mitch all chuckled as they were pulled into the principal's office.

It wasn't one of Carter's finest moments, but he did stick up for his family. After all, that's what Eve and Mitch were to him.

He looked up to see Eve coming out of the doctor's office with a smile on her face. "Well?"

"She says I'm fine." She started walking towards the door, but he reached out and took her hand, halting her.

"Eve?" He waited until she looked at him. "What did she say was triggering the blackouts?"

She took a deep breath. "I'll tell you everything she said over lunch."

How could he argue with that? He'd been in the waiting room for almost two hours. Taking her hand in his, they walked back out to the car. "I know this great seafood place just down the street."

They sat in the packed restaurant in a booth overlooking the cove and enjoyed clam chowder together.

He waited for her to tell him what the doctor had said. He knew that the more he pushed her to tell him, the longer it would take her to spit it out. Finally, when his bowl was almost empty, she set her spoon down.

"First off, she wanted me to have another CAT scan. That's what took so long. Anyway, she said pretty much the same thing that the doctor in Chicago said. It will take time to recover. I will have headaches, blurred vision, etc. etc." She took a drink of her water and he knew she was purposely leaving out the part he was waiting to hear. He looked at her until, finally, she sighed and looked back.

"She doesn't know why I'm blacking out. She thinks it could just be a side effect each time I remember something. She doesn't want me using heavy equipment, yadda yadda."

He thought about it. "Has she ever seen a case like this? After all, she is a specialist that handles head injuries."

"Yes and no. She's seen plenty of amnesia cases, but none of them have blacked out upon triggering a memory." She looked at him and he could see the fear in her eyes for the first time. "Honestly, it makes me want to stop trying to remember anything."

He reached across the table and took her hand. "Don't worry, I'll be here. We'll take it easy. You've been doing too much around the house." He frowned and thought about all the stuff he'd allowed her to help with the last few days.

"Carter, I've barely lifted a finger. Besides, there isn't much more to do. It's not like I can go back to work. I don't even know if I still know how to do my job." This time she frowned.

He wanted to laugh. "Eve trusts me, your job isn't something you'd forget how to do."

"What do you mean?"

"Well, the majority of your work is to wine and dine new clients and get them to sign a contract. Then…"—he raised his shoulders and lowered them again— "…well, you just take care of them when they need something. All marketing and other promotions for the clients are handled by the special teams in the office. You're the company's biggest asset, though," he said quickly when she started to frown again. "You play a huge part in our business, not to mention the fact that you've basically been running every-thing, including Mitch and myself." He smiled, remembering how she was able to talk or argue him into anything.

She was silent most of the drive back to the house. The snow was falling more quickly now, and he was thankful the men had finished with the new roof. There was still so much he wanted to get done, but he was taking it in stages. He was planning on spending more time at the place in the future. He might even move up there. Mitchell and Sandi had bought a large place just down the coast from him. They planned on living there full-time after their wedding next spring.

Maybe he and Eve would make this their permanent place as well. It wasn't as if they couldn't move the business up here and still be successful. Honestly, he thought they could run the place from anywhere and still be successful, thanks to Eve.

He smiled to himself when he realized he'd started thinking of them being together as a couple. The only thing looming over his head now was her health and the possibility that her memory would return, and they'd be back to square one. Friendship.

When they made it back to the house, Eve retreated up to their room. Since that first night they'd spent together, he'd moved into the large room with her. She didn't mind; after all, according to him, they were getting married and she knew she had feelings for him that ran deep. She enjoyed the physical relationship with him and the tender nights spent in his arms. But needing some alone time, she slipped into the bathroom and started the water. He must have gotten the clue because the entire time she soaked her worries away in the tub, he didn't come in, even though the door was unlocked.

Hearing the doctor's worried attitude today stirred up her own worries. Was she going to spend the rest of her life passing out every time she remembered something? The doctor had ruled out brain damage, but that didn't mean there wasn't something else going on. Something mental. The specialist had hinted that it was psychological and that she should see a shrink. She'd even given her a card for a psychologist. She didn't need to see anyone to have them tell her she was stressed. Staying in the big house was relaxing, being with Carter felt right, but the rest of her world was black. It was almost as if nothing existed beyond the walls of the house and the waters of the cove.

Maybe she should head back to the city. Back to her own apartment in New York. Would she find peace of mind there? Would there be clues as to who she was now, instead of all the old memories she saw around the place here?

Staying here, she felt like she was trapped in an old rerun of a show. Seeing the younger images of herself and Carter didn't explain how their relationship had advanced to what it is today. Nor did it explain her personality and style. She'd been doing a lot of thinking about going back to the city and when she finally pulled herself out of the tub she thought she'd come to a decision. Quickly dressing in a pair of her black leggings and a large sweater. She put on a pair of fluffy pink socks that had been in her suitcase from Chicago. Walking down the stairs, she was surprised to find the living room in darkness with only a few candles and a fire in the fireplace to light the otherwise dark room. Candles and two plate settings sat on the coffee table next to a gorgeous chocolate cake that had one sparkler candle on it. Carter stood on the other side of the table smiling.

"What's all this?" She walked all the way into the room.

"I thought we'd celebrate your clean bill of health. I felt like baking and I know how much you love chocolate." He motioned to the couch and she walked over and sat. Just knowing that he'd gone through all the trouble made her want him. She couldn't imagine another man baking a cake for her. No wonder they were together. All of the doubts she had about their relationship went out the door at that moment.

She walked over and sat on the newly reupholstered couch that had been delivered the day before. Now it was as good looking as it was comfortable.

When she looked at the cake, something told her he was right about her loving chocolate. Her mouth began to water as she looked at the chocolate mass before her, and the thought of eating half the cake herself popped into her head.

"I found this." He held up a movie case and shook it. "Your all-time favorite."

"What?" She tried to see the name of the movie. She watched him frown a little.

"Say Anything." He walked over and pushed it into the VHS player.

She thought about it and shook her head. "Doesn't ring a bell."

"That's okay. It will be like watching it for the first time." He walked over, sat next to her, and started cutting the cake, giving her a large slice, then putting one of equal size on his plate. "I know it's not kosher to have cake for dinner, but since we had a late lunch, I didn't think you'd mind."

She took a bite and closed her eyes. Something sparked in her mind, but there was no dizziness, no feeling faint. Instead, warmth spread throughout her entire body. She'd felt the exact same way a few times in the last few days, always in the arms of Carter as they made love.

"Mmmm, oh my." She licked her lips and watched his eyes heat. "I can definitely say that chocolate cake is still my favorite."

"It's becoming my favorite as well." He watched her very closely. She couldn't explain it, but she felt a strange sensation pulsing through her knowing she had so much power over him. She watched as he picked up his fork and took a bite of the moist cake. His tongue darted out and licked the icing from his lips. Desire shot through her so quickly her head spun, and she gripped the table to stop the shaking she felt.

"Eve?" Just her name on his lips did something to her. That voice. The smoothness, the richness of it.

She nodded her head, showing him that she felt the same way. Slowly he set his plate down, then took hers from her. When he reached for her, she held onto his biceps and let him pull her closer.

His mouth was warm and his hands roamed over her back as she arched towards him. She felt like no matter what she did, she couldn't get close enough. Hoisting herself up, she straddled his hips as he leaned back on the couch. Her hands went to his hair and held his mouth to hers.

His hands were under her sweater, running up and down her sides, and then he was pulling her sweater up and over her head. She leaned back and watched his face as he looked at her. She saw the surprise and heat cross his face as he noticed that she'd worn nothing else underneath. Then he dipped his head and placed his mouth on her taut skin, running his lips over the tender buds.

"Carter." She couldn't stop herself from moaning his name. She wanted to feel him next to her. Leaning back, she pulled off his shirt in one quick motion. He smiled a little as she ran her hands over his pecs. "Have I told you I really, really enjoy this body of yours?" She smiled and leaned down to follow the path her fingers had taken with her mouth. He moaned and leaned his head back against the couch cushions as his hands ran over her bare shoulders and back. Then she leaned up and ran her skin over his, chest to chest, skin to skin, as she took his mouth and enjoyed his lips again.

Abruptly, Carter stood, picking her up with him. He turned and laid her down gently on the couch, following her down. He hovered over her as he looked into her eyes. She reached up and pulled him back to her, wrapping her legs around his hips. She felt his desire pressed up against her, the coarse material of his jeans rubbing against the softness of her leggings. His hips moved in a slow motion as his mouth tortured her. His hands moved over the light material, pulling it aside as his fingers found her sensitive skin. She arched back and moaned as he rubbed her gently, causing her hips to start moving and rotating. Then he pushed her leggings down off her legs, taking his time as he pulled each foot free.

She tried to reach down for his jean's zipper, but he just

held her hands still. "Let me. I want to enjoy all of you," he said against her skin.

"Carter, I need you." She tried to get free from his light grasp. "Now, I need you now." She moved her hips against him and felt him hold still as she rubbed herself against him. He released her hands and she made her way towards his zipper, pushing his jeans off his hips, enjoying the muscles as she pushed them lower.

She felt his skin next to hers and moaned. His legs were still trapped in the jeans, but she enjoyed running her hands over his tight butt, pulling him closer to her.

"Eve?" He tried to pull back. "Wait." He reached around and pulled out a condom. Quickly donning it, he returned to her and took the kiss deeper as he slid into her. She wrapped her legs around his hips and held on. Just when she thought she couldn't wait any longer for him, he kissed the underside of her ear and whispered that he loved her as she threw her head back and screamed his name.

arter lay there listening to his heart beat rapidly in his ears. He tried to hold his breath and lower the banging in his ears. He desperately wanted to hear her, to see if she'd been as moved as he had. To hear her response, if she'd had any.

Finally, what seemed like minutes later, he heard her say his name. Leaning back, he looked down into her face and knew she had recovered more quickly than he had. It took just a second for him to slide his jeans back up and on.

The movie played on the set as the fire died in the hearth. He walked over and threw a couple more logs on it, stirring it until it was crackling again. Then he walked over and hit the rewind button, to start the movie again. When it was ready to start again, he turned towards her and smiled. She was dressed again, her legs tucked up under her on the couch.

"I know this is all new to you. Us." He motioned between them, waving his hands. "So, I've tried to go slow, but I can't deny my feelings. I won't deny them. I know you need some more time to work things out. I just wanted you to know how I felt." He smiled and walked over to sit next to her. "Now, how about we eat some cake and watch your favorite movie?"

She nodded and smiled at him, leaving so much unsaid.

He fell asleep halfway through the movie. They'd ended up laying down, him behind her on the couch. The warmth and the feel of her heartbeat next to him made him drift right off.

The dream started at normal speed. Them in the bar, dancing to the Irish music. Kissing on the dance floor as their bodies rubbed up against each other. Then they left, and he turned back to get his cell phone. He screamed in his head not to leave her alone, but his dream self-continued to jog happily into the bar. He had a relieved look on his face when he picked up his cell phone, the two-hundred-dollar item that had caused so much pain.

Here's where everything slowed down and deviated from reality. Next, he was in the alley, watching Eve fight off a black blob that was her attacker. It was two sizes bigger than he was and had no mass. He watched sheer terror cross her face. She looked around for him but couldn't see him as he tried to run towards her, screaming. Then the beast struck, and she screamed his name.

He woke and sat straight up, almost dislodging Eve in the process.

"What?" Her eyes flew open. "What is it?" She looked around as he began to feel the tension leave his body.

"Sorry," he pulled her closer so that she wouldn't end up on the floor. "It was just a bad dream." He kissed her hair and noticed the snow was really coming down outside. He felt her shiver. "We should head upstairs. I can get a fire going up there."

"Hmmm." She settled back down against his chest. "I like it down here. Besides, I know how we could get a little of our own heat working for us." She trailed kisses along his collarbone, running her hands under his shirt in the process. He leaned back and let her enjoy herself.

She removed his shirt slowly, then her own more quickly. When he reached up and touched her, she leaned her head back and moaned, her hair spilling over her back as he ran his hands over her soft skin. When she leaned forward, her dark hair spilled over them, encasing them in a private world. He could smell the sweet scent from her shampoo and reached up to touch her hair. It was silky soft, and he pushed it up over her ear so he could see her eyes. She was wiggling, trying to get out of her leggings, and when he reached down to help her, she took his wrists in her hands and pulled them over his head. "No, let me." She stood up and pulled them down, then leaned over and unzipped his jeans, her eyes on his. She smiled when she noticed his fists clenched by his sides.

Sliding his jeans down his hips, she took her time as she pulled them off of his legs. Then she stood over him and just looked at him.

"You really have a wonderful body." He could barely see her face in the darkness of the room. The fire embers cast a light glow, enough that she had a halo around her form.

"Right back at ya." He smiled as she leaned over and started running her hands along his legs, up his hips, until he held his breath. Then she ran one hand over his chest as the other wrapped around his length, causing his eyes to close. His hips jerked as she started to move up and down him while her other hand ran over his stomach muscles.

"Eve!" He gasped after several seconds had gone by. "Please." He kept his eyes closed and his hands in fists above his head where she'd left them.

He heard her hunting around and peaked out to see her grabbing a package from his back pocket. Closing his eyes again, he felt her tentative hands as she wrapped him in protection.

He felt the couch cushions dip as she moved over him, his hands went to her hips as she slid slowly onto him. He looked up at her. Her dark hair was over her chest, and the curls bounced as she swayed on him. He reached up and took her breasts in his hands, enjoying the feel of her hair on the back of his hands. Gently, he rubbed his fingers over her nipples and watched her head fall back and her eyes slide closed.

Her motion slowed as she enjoyed the feel of him touching her. His other hand went to her hips to guide her, to keep the pace going. He sat up and gently pushed her hair aside and placed his mouth on her skin, sucking gently, until the peak rolled in his mouth. He felt her hips moving faster now on their own. Her heated skin rubbed up against his until they both cried out blindly.

When he lay back down, she went with him and he pulled the blanket from the back of the couch over them both. He could hear her breathing steady as he lay there and thought about his next move.

❄

The next few days, the snow continued to fall. There was a brisk breeze coming off the water, so they spent a lot of time inside. Finally, on the fourth day, the sun came out and they went on a short walk. She hadn't had any other episodes since their trip to Portland. She knew it was just a matter of time.

Carter was trying to keep her mind off of it by filling her time with him. They spent a lot of time working on the house. He painted, she watched. They did get into town to get supplies once and ate at a local restaurant, The Shepherd's Pie. It was in an old red brick building that had large dark windows and a gold sign above the door. The place was crowded when they entered, and she felt warm and right at home. It was hard to explain, but it just felt right. Carter had told her it was a place they'd been going to since they were kids. Several of the guests greeted her by name. She quietly nodded and answered their concerned questions. Evidently, word had spread throughout the small town that she was ill. Everyone said they were happy she was feeling better. She got the hint that no one really knew what was wrong with her. She wanted to keep it that way and Carter picked up on it and kept her secret.

Carter cooked every meal, cleaned the house regularly, and did laundry. She wondered if he was like this all the time or just since she'd lost her memory. If he was, why on earth hadn't she married him years ago?

They walked to the edge of the water and stood and watched the choppy water hit the dark rocks. He pulled her close and held onto her as they swayed in the cold breeze. When she shivered, he suggested they head back. As they were walking up to the house, they saw a dark sedan sitting in the drive.

Carter frowned and grabbed her hand. "I hope you're ready for this," he mumbled.

"What?" She tried to pull him to a stop. He just shook his head.

"Best to wait and see." They entered the house and she saw a man and a woman sitting at the kitchen table, enjoying a cup of coffee. The man was in full military uniform, his hat sat on the edge of the table. He was thin and clean-shaven and completely bald. The woman looked smaller, and her dark curly hair, her olive skin, and her deep-set eyes reminded Eve so much of her own.

Eve tightened her grip on Carter's hand as they walked into the room.

"Oh, here they are now." Her mother stood and looked at them, and her father followed. They stood like statues across the room, waiting for permission to move. There was no rushing across the room, grabbing their daughter in an emotional embrace. A few seconds of awkward silence passed, and she would have settled for a nod or any form of greeting.

"Hel—Hello." She said as Carter pulled her farther into the room.

"Mr. and Mrs. Taylor, I'm happy you received my messages." Carter stopped at the end of the table, Eve's hand still tightly in his.

"What is that you are wearing?" her mother asked, a sour look on her face. Eve looked down and realized she'd put on her leggings and Carter's sweatshirt on over a shirt. She'd worn one of his grandfather's old jackets to the beach, but they'd pulled their coats off at the doorway.

"It's Carter's," she said absently as she looked between the pair.

"It's true then?" her father asked. His voice wasn't familiar to her, nor was her mother's, as she'd hoped they'd be. After all, there must have been some time when she'd been a child that he'd read to her, comforted her when she'd been ill or had fallen. But when they spoke, there wasn't a hint of familiarity in their tones.

"What?" She sat when Carter pulled out a chair for her. Her parents sat again and resumed drinking their coffee. She watched Carter walk into the kitchen and pull out two more cups for them. Then she turned back towards her parents.

"That you don't remember anything?" her mother added.

Eve nodded her head in agreement. "Yes."

Her father sighed. "I suppose you'll need to come home with us."

It sounded to her like she'd be putting them out like she was going to be a burden to them.

She shook her head. "No." The thought of going with this couple scared her. She couldn't explain it, but her hands started to shake, and her palms got sweaty. "I'm not going anywhere. I'm where I need to be."

"Well, honey, I don't think you're in your right mind to make that decision," her mother said in a sweet tone. "I think your father knows what's best. If he says you'll need to come home with us, then you and I will need to go upstairs and pack your belongings." Her mother started to get up.

"I'm not going anywhere," Eve said more firmly.

Her father slammed his fist down on the table. "I thought you'd gotten rid of that attitude when you lost your memory. Now I see it's embedding in that skull of yours.

You will do exactly what we say this time around. These people have corrupted you far too much. It's high time we took you in hand and straightened you out."

Eve stood, her hands fisted on the table, and said in the calmest voice she could muster. "Since I woke up over four weeks ago, I've been treated with the utmost kindness. I've been taken in by people I deemed to be strangers. People not related to me who've shown me such kindness, that there was no doubt as to their intentions. Four weeks I've sat here waiting for my family to come and show me some of the same. Now you're standing here in my kitchen, dictating what I must do." She felt herself vibrating with anger. "I see no concern for my health in your eyes or in the way you talk to me. And you have the gall to stand there and tell me what to do." She shook her head. "Out. I want you out of my house, both of you. And until you decide you want to be my parents and not just in control, you can stay gone. I know who my family is, and none of them are blood-related." She turned and walked out of the room without another word.

She grabbed the jacket from the rack as she walked out the back door. She didn't know where she was heading, just that she needed the cold air on her face. When she hit the beach, she turned and continued to walk at a brisk pace. Her eyesight blurred as tears streamed down her face.

Carter had warned her; he'd told her that she wasn't close to her parents. She should have expected something like this, but in her mind, she kept playing fairytale scenes of her mother and father coming in, engulfing her in their arms as they cried for her lost memories.

Now she was the one left crying. When she'd walked

farther then she'd ever gone, she stopped and wiped her face. Her vision was blurry and her head was pounding. The weather had held, but the breeze was cold as it came off the sound. She looked around and took several large breaths. How could she have gotten her hopes up so much?

Had they always been like that? No wonder she'd bonded with two boys from school. No wonder she'd adopted someone else's family as her own.

She stood there, her arms crossed over her chest for warmth, enjoying the cold breeze when she heard a noise behind her. Turning, she thought maybe Carter had followed her to the beach but looking around she didn't see anyone. Since her vision was blurry she could barely make out the tree line a few feet away. Maybe he was there, coming towards her, but she just wasn't able to see him.

Using the jacket arms, she wiped her eyes, trying to see better. She heard a branch break and looked up again. This time, she could see movement, but her eyes were still so out of focus she couldn't make out the form. Was it her father that had followed her?

"Hello?" she called out and waited for a response. The howling of the breeze was at her back, but she listened for anything, anyone calling back to her. "Carter?" She waited and heard another snap of a branch, then the dark figure started moving slowly towards her. Taking a step back, she watched as a dark blurry figure appeared from the edge of the trees, less than a yard from her.

CHAPTER 12

Carter paced up and down the front porch. "Stupid!" He barked. "How stupid am I to let her run off like that? Doesn't she know better than to take off?" He stopped and looked across the snow-covered ground of the front yard. He'd tried to follow her footprints in the snow, but when he'd arrived at the beach, it had been empty, so he'd returned home. Now, panic set in and he looked down at his cell phone for the hundredth time since she'd disappeared. Should he call the police?

What if she got lost? What if she had another episode? He stormed down the front porch just as she came bolting from the trees, fear on her face.

He caught her when she launched herself into his arms. "Eve?" He ran his hands down her hair and just held onto her. All thoughts of scolding her about running off flew from his mind. "What is it?"

He looked around, towards the woods where she'd come from, looking for anything.

"There was someone. On the beach." She said into his chest.

He felt like laughing. "It is a public beach, honey. There are a few other houses around here. Maybe someone else went for a walk." He kissed the top of her head as she shook her head.

"No, they stood just out of sight and watched me. He was breaking the branches on purpose, making that sound because he knew I couldn't see him."

He tensed, then pulled her face up towards his. He could see a headache and tell her vision was almost gone. "How bad?" He asked.

She shook her head, again. "I'm fine."

"No, you're not. How bad?" He asked again.

She pulled back and rubbed her temples. "Bad. I was crying, and I think it triggered a migraine, like the first few days."

He gathered her up and started walking towards the house. "You have a few pills left. I'll heat some clam chowder up and you'll rest."

"Carter," she said when they were back inside, and he'd set her on the couch and tucked her under the large knit blanket. "There really was someone watching me."

"You're safe here." He leaned down and kissed her. "Your parents have gone. No one is going to make you do anything you don't want to." He smiled and started to walk from the room, turning the light down as he went out. He turned to watch her rest her head back against the couch pillow.

Then he went into the kitchen and pulled out the Tupperware with the leftover clam chowder he'd made last week. As he heated it up, he went to all the doors and windows on the main floor and made sure they were locked. He didn't doubt that she'd seen someone but felt that it had probably been one of their neighbors. *Their* neighbors. He liked the sound of that. When she'd stood up to her parents, she'd called the place her house. He liked the sound of that, too. As far as he was concerned, it belonged to all three of them: Mitch, Eve, and him. Really, it was the only true home any of them had ever known.

He walked back into the living room with a tray of hot soup, a glass of water, and her pills and watched as she ate the entire bowl while he downed his own. Then she took her pills and rested her head back against the pillows.

"Have they always been like that?" She kept her eyes closed and he knew she was fighting the migraine.

"Yes. Our senior year they accused Mitch and myself of sexually molesting you. They thought of our family here as a cult, that we'd brainwashed you. They even tried to file a lawsuit to keep you away from here."

She opened her eyes and looked at him. "What happened?"

He chuckled, remembering how determined she was in her youth. "You ran away and ended up here, of course. My grandfather threatened to sue your parents for slander. After all, that's what he'd done for a living. He was one of Maine's finest attorneys." He chuckled. "That's the last time you lived with them. You stayed here until you graduated school, then went off to college with the rest of us."

She leaned her head back and closed her eyes again. "Thank you, Carter."

"For what?" He ran her hair through his fingers.

"For being my family." She leaned over and rested her head on his chest and fell asleep. He sat there, watching the fire die, listening to her steady breathing as he thought about their future.

The next morning, he called Mitch. He'd been in contact with him a few times during the hiatus, but he knew it was time he made a visit. Mitch and Sandi were heading up there this weekend to see them, to be there for Eve.

He busied himself with cleaning the place, finishing the office and keeping Eve happy and entertained. Her headache stuck around for two days, during which time he would barely allow her off the couch. Even watching TV ended up being too much for her, so he'd talk to her, tell her stories like he used to do when the three of them had been a team.

She'd told him that when he talked to her, it helped soothe the pain. So he relayed all the stories his grandpa and uncles used to tell him. Even some that he and Mitch had made up as kids, scary stories that they would tell each other during sleepovers.

He left her alone only once after that day when he'd driven into town to get some supplies. He didn't want to take her because she was still having some vision problems. When he returned home, every light in the place was on as he drove up. He knew something was wrong. Since her parents' visit, her eyes had been very sensitive to light and he'd kept all the lights on dim or off during the day. He jumped from the car and raced to the door.

Eve watched Carter drive away down the bumpy lane and wished her head didn't hurt so much so she could go with him. Even though he was just going into the local store to get supplies, it was getting out, doing something. It had been almost a week since she'd left the place. Not that she was complaining; he'd done a wonderful job of keeping her entertained when she wasn't feeling well. She stood by the window in the darkened room and watched as snow started to fall again. Her vision was still so bad that all she could really make out were white specks floating down. She found it quite beautiful to watch. Turning away, she decided a hot bath would help her relax and maybe she could convince her body and her eyes to work properly again.

The water and jets felt great and did a good job relaxing her, but when she walked out of the restroom, there on the bed was a red rose, its petals ripped from the bud and thrown across the white comforter, looking a lot like blood. The stem was left twisted and looked like a dead limb as it lay next to the petals.

"Carter?" She walked to the bedroom door and called downstairs. Why would he leave the stem there? Was he trying to be romantic? When she received no reply, she walked to the window and looked out towards the parking area. His car wasn't there. Her breath started to hitch, and she turned back towards the door when she heard a floorboard creak outside her door. "Carter?" She gripped the windowsill with both hands, leaning against the cool glass.

She heard the stairs creak and rushed to the hallway to look over the railing. A dark figure rushed from the bottom step as she leaned over and looked down. She rushed back to her room and was about to slam the door shut and lock it when she heard the front door slam. Rushing to the window, she watched the figure rush past the woodpile and into the trees. Just as he approached the trees, he stopped and looked back. She blinked a few times, trying to convince her eyes to work so she could make out a face, but it was too far away, and her eyesight hadn't returned to normal.

Then the figure dodged into the trees, she rushed downstairs and quickly locked the doors, turning on every light in the house as she went. She grabbed the fireplace poker, the only weapon she could think of and sat at the kitchen door, waiting for Carter to return.

What seemed to her like hours later, Carter's face appeared on the other side of the glass door. He tried the handle and she rushed forward to unlock the deadbolt. When she threw open the door, she threw herself at him, a fireplace poker and all.

It took half an hour for the local police to come out and remove the flower petals as evidence. They checked the trees around the house, and upon finding nothing but some muddy footprints that could belong to anyone, they left.

Carter sat across from her at the table as they ate cold turkey sandwiches. She could have sworn he was mad, but when she asked, he would mumble that he was deep in thought. That night they slept on the couch, falling asleep to *Bill and Ted's Excellent Adventure*, one of Carter's favorite movies. She just couldn't bring herself to sleep on the bed knowing that someone had touched it, had been in that room. At least not yet, anyway.

The next day, Sandi and Mitch arrived and upon seeing them, her headache disappeared completely. She hugged Mitch like she meant it this time, instead of as if he was a stranger. She'd seen the pictures, and after meeting her parents, knew that pictures and her life couldn't lie. Mitch had been like her brother and she needed to treat him like family.

He hugged her back and kissed her forehead. She felt warm and knew she was loved. Sandi cried a little when she saw her.

"I'm so happy that you're doing better. We've been wanting to come up sooner." She looked over at Carter.

Eve turned to Carter. "Carter?"

"I thought you needed the rest." He smiled and put an arm around her.

"It's okay, really. We've been so busy with work and planning the wedding." Sandi took her arm and walked her into the living room.

Eve remembered Carter telling her that Sandi and Mitch had stayed here last year. Sandi looked comfortable in the house.

"Oh, you got a new sofa?" Sandi frowned a little.

"No," Eve looked across the room. "We had it reupholstered. Same sofa, new look."

"Oh, good. I've never sat or slept on a more comfortable couch." Sandi walked over and sighed as she sat on the large cushions. "Yes, same couch." She patted the cushion next to her. "Come, I'll tell you everything you've missed while you've been away."

That night, Eve and Carter slept in his room down the hall and gave Sandi and Mitch the master bedroom. Carter had made lasagna for dinner and Sandi had helped by making an Indian side dish that was hot and spicy. Eve found she not only like it, she knew without a doubt that she loved Indian food. Sandi promised to show her how to cook when she came back to the city.

"I like Sandi," Eve said against Carter's chest as they

lay in the bed looking up at the ceiling. "Were we friends before?"

"Hmm," Carter said. "Yes, actually, she was a client to you before. You knew her as Samantha Rain, the pseudonym she used to hide from her family."

Something flashed in Eve's mind. This time there was no pain, no blacking out. She saw with clarity Sandi, with longer hair, sitting across from her at a table, laughing. She was showing her a painting of red flowers with white circles behind them. Then the memory was gone.

Eve sat up and looked down at Carter. "I just had a memory."

He sat up quickly, grabbing hold of her. "How's your head? Do you feel dizzy?" He started to hold her.

"No, I'm fine. No sharp pain, no blurry vision, nothing." She smiled. "I remembered Sandi when you mentioned the name Samantha Rain." She blinked a few times. "I remember meeting her at a cafe. I think it was called Hell's Kitchen Cafe. Oh my God! I remember something else. A couple months ago I swore off eating meat." She glared at him. "I told you this. I told you I was becoming a vegetarian and you've fed me meat this whole time." She slapped his shoulder as he laughed, and she thought about how she'd get back at him later.

"We never thought you'd stick to it. It did last a couple months, though." He pulled her back into his arms. "I'm happy you're starting to remember. I think having your family near you is helping."

She was still steaming about him breaking her diet, but his arms felt too wonderful to be mad for long. She melted back into his arms and enjoyed the rest of the night.

CHAPTER 13

itch and Sandi's stay helped keep Eve entertained, and small pieces of her memory were coming back without her blacking out. Each time she remembered more, Carter got nervous thinking she'd realize they hadn't been a couple like he'd hinted at.

So far, he was still safe. Sandi and Eve had talked wedding while he and Mitch had finished working on painting all the rooms upstairs. Carter told Mitch about everything that had happened since they'd arrived—her parents visit, the break-in, how Eve had been passing out.

"I don't like it." Mitch stopped painting and frowned. "We still don't know if she was attacked on purpose or it was a random thing. Carter, there could be someone after her."

He stopped and looked at his friend. "Like a stalker?"

"Yeah, just like a stalker. Sandi has been helping out while Eve is gone. She was using her office and she noticed a pile of letters in Eve's desk. At first, Sandi thought they were from Steve, but shortly after she started helping out, she received another one. Sandi opened the mail thinking it was from a client. Carter, there were threats and some scary shit in there." Mitch looked towards the door, no doubt not wanting Sandi to hear him cursing or for Eve to hear about the threatening letters. Either way, Mitch's voice got lower and he walked closer to Carter. "Well, I found the stack of letters and after reading them, turned a copy of them over to the Chicago police. They assured me it had nothing to do with her attack. They claimed it was a bum that frequented that alleyway, stealing clothing so he could keep warm. They told me that he most likely wanted her coat. Anyway, after what you've just told me, I'm inclined to think that this creep knows she's here."

"Who knows I'm here?" Eve stood just inside the door, her face a little pale.

Carter dropped his paintbrush in the bucket and walked over to her. "No one. Mitch and I were just chatting about a client."

She yanked her arm out of his. "You're lying." She looked at Mitch. "It's written all over his face. I don't know how I know it, but I know you're lying to me."

Carter glared at Mitch. "You never could lie to her, bro."

"Sorry," Mitch grumbled and set his paintbrush down. "Maybe we should tell her."

"Why? What good would it do?" Carter asked. Mitch shrugged his shoulders.

Eve stood, her arms crossed over her chest. They both knew that look. She wasn't going to budge until she heard it all.

"Fine!" He threw up his hands and they proceeded to tell her what they knew.

After they were done, Eve walked from the room without a word. Carter tracked her down in their room. She was packing her clothes up.

"What do you think you're doing?" He started removing her clothes from her bag.

"I'm going to return to the city with Mitch and Sandi. I think it's time I stopped hiding out. Besides, I'm having more memories and no fainting spells." She stopped and glared at him as he tossed her clothes back into the drawers.

"You're not better. Just two days ago you could barely see." He closed her empty suitcase.

She stood there with her arms crossed and glared at him. "Are you telling me I can't go back to the city?"

"Yes. No! I mean…" He knew he'd stuck his foot in it now. "You can do whatever you want. I'm not forcing you to stay. I'm just concerned, that's all." He walked up to her and rubbed her arms with his hands, then watched her slowly relax under his touch. "Give it a few more days. Then we'll head back together." She thought about it for a while.

"Well, I guess a few more days here with you won't be so bad." She smiled. He didn't know if it was the shock of actually winning his first argument with her or the fact that Mitch was standing in the doorway laughing, but he was slow to react when she punched him in the gut. She'd never hit very hard; Mitch and he had always said she fought like a girl. He was thankful for it at the moment.

"What was that for?" He winced and rubbed his stomach.

"Just a friendly reminder. Don't think for a moment that you can ever tell me what I can and can't do." She smiled and patted his cheek as she turned to walk out. She stopped by Mitch then balled her fist and punched him in the shoulder.

"Ouch, what was that for?" Mitch asked as he rubbed his shoulder.

"That was for letting this jackass"—she pointed back towards Carter— "talk you into staying away so long." Then she punched him again on the other shoulder.

"Stop it." Mitch frowned and rubbed his other shoulder. "What was that one for?"

"That was for keeping secrets from me." She leaned up and placed a kiss on his cheek. "That was for being my friend." She turned and walked out of the room.

"Hey, I didn't get a kiss!" Carter raced after her as Mitch laughed.

That evening they all sat around the fireplace chatting about the good old days. Mitch had some funny stories about when they were kids. Sandi said something about wishing she could have seen it when Eve thought of the picture album. Jumping up, she raced up to their room and looked around.

She hadn't seen the photo album since the first week they'd been there. Finally, she found it under Carter's travel bag. When she pulled the photo book out, his bag dumped out and she bent down to pick up everything that had fallen out. In the pile was a folder. There was a yellow sticky note attached to it with her name on it and written beside it was a large amount of money.

She stopped what she was doing and started to read. Fifteen minutes later she walked downstairs. The photo book in her hands was almost forgotten. She handed the book to Sandi who immediately started looking through the old photos.

Carter stood and took her shoulders. She jerked back and walked into the kitchen, knowing he would follow her.

"What? What is it? Did you have another spell?" He asked, trying to hold her still.

She turned on him. "What's this?" She held up the paperwork.

He looked at it like it was a snake she was holding. "Nothing." He tried to reach for it.

"No." She pulled it out of his reach. "Too late. Tell me why I was buying into a company I thought I was already a partner of. Better yet, tell me why I'd have to buy into a company owned by people I deemed were my family, at all?" Her voice was slightly raised.

"Eve, listen. I can explain." He started to walk towards her.

"Stop!" She tossed the paperwork towards him. "From where I'm standing, you're no better than my parents. You've lied to me. You made me believe you had my best interest at heart, that you cared." Her voice hitched. "That I was more to you than numbers." She glared at him.

"Eve, you've got it all wrong." He was trying to walk towards her again.

"Really? From where I'm standing, I see a man who told me we were getting married, yet when I talked to Sandi, she knew nothing about our engagement. I brushed it off as maybe we hadn't told anyone yet. You told me I was a partner in your business, now I find these"—she pointed to the paperwork on the floor— "that say I was paying my two best friends, whom I've been told were my family, to become partners. In my book, family doesn't do that. Family doesn't exploit family, Carter. So tell me why I was having to pay. Then maybe you can tell me why one amount, the lower of the two, was crossed out and a higher one was put in its place. Did you find out I had more money? Did you want to take every cent from me?" Her head was throbbing now and all she wanted to do was retreat to a quiet room and cry.

"Eve, I can explain," he said for the third time. When she looked into his eyes, she knew he was about to lie to her. Tossing up her hands, she stormed from the room.

"Save it. I don't want to hear anything," she said over her shoulder as she marched to her room to pack. She hadn't seen this coming. Her mind just refused to believe anything other than she was being used. Had Mitch known about this as well? She was at the base of the stairs and decided to find out, but when she walked to the doorway, Mitch and Sandi were in a warm embrace and she lost the heart. Instead, she went up the stairs to finish packing. Mitch and Sandi were leaving to drive back to New York after breakfast; she'd just make sure she was going with them.

Two days later, Mitch and Sandi walked her up to her apartment. When she opened the door, she was shocked. The sheer size of the place was something she wasn't prepared for. The fact that it was extremely well decorated and that she immediately felt a warmth spread through her when she walked in made her realize she'd made the right choice in coming back to the city.

It wasn't that she'd broken things off with Carter; she'd tried to talk to him the evening before she left and had explained that she needed some space. He'd just looked at her like she'd kicked him and nodded.

When Mitch and Sandi left, Eve walked around her apartment looking at everything. Here there were newer pictures of her with Carter and Mitch, some even with Sandi. She noticed there wasn't one picture of her parents.

The hardwood floors looked new throughout the place. The light-colored furniture was very appealing, but when she sat down on the leather couch, she instantly missed the big soft one in Maine.

The view out her large windows was breathtaking. The evening sky sparkled with a million lights as the snow gently fell. Her apartment was on the twenty-second floor and she knew that the view in daylight would be just as breathtaking.

Walking towards her bedroom, she stopped at a small office filled with fabric. Walking in, she realized they were clothes that she must have made. She took her time and assessed every item. She also had sketches of designs. She walked over to a large rack full of finished items. They were very good. Smiling, she realized she had a hidden talent that even Mitch and Carter hadn't known about. Then she started wondering if she still had the talent, or if it was lost with all her other memories.

Straightening her shoulders, she was determined to find out more about herself now, and she knew just where to start: with her job. Even though Mitch had tried to convince her that she didn't need to rush it, she was determined to make it into the office in the morning.

Walking into her bedroom, she started unpacking her clothes from her suitcases. In her huge walk-in closet, she found a mixture of clothing she'd made and some she'd purchased. There was everything from formal to very casual, all of which she found very appealing and to her taste.

Sitting on the edge of her bed, she looked in each drawer of her nightstand. She found a diary and decided to get comfortable by sitting back and started reading to learn about herself. When she was sure she was nice and comfortable, she opened the small book and read the first line and felt like crying.

"I think I'm in love with Carter."

Carter watched Eve walk into the office that next morning. The tight black skirt clung to every curve, and the bright blouse called for every man to look at her chest, which was presented beautifully. The gold earrings matched the bracelets and necklace she wore; they'd been a gift from him and Mitch when they'd still been in college.

Eve hadn't known it, but Carter had followed them all the way back to New York. He'd tried to stay out of sight the entire trip, but Mitch had shown up at his place shortly after he'd gotten home.

Eve looked a little intimidated. He could tell she was trying to hide it, but just the way she held her shoulders told him she felt uncomfortable. Lesley, Eve's secretary, greeted her at the elevators with a cup of coffee. Everyone in the office had been warned about Eve's condition and told they should treat her the same, with a few minor adjustments.

"Good morning Eve, I'm Lesley, your personal

assistant. I've got your morning messages and meetings all lined up for you. Just let me know if you're not feeling up to something, and we can always reschedule." Lesley was in her early twenties, short and very blonde. She was a whirlwind of efficiency, just like Eve wanted. Now, however, Eve was looking at her like she was too much to handle. Carter chose that moment to step out of his office door and wave off Lesley.

"Eve? Would you mind coming into my office for a few minutes?" He turned and waited for her to follow him in. He noticed her chin went up slightly as she walked towards him. He also saw heat come into her eyes.

Shutting the door behind him, he motioned for her to sit. When she did, he walked around and sat on the edge of his desk, looking down at her.

"How are you feeling?" He'd been dying to know if she'd missed him as much as he'd missed her last night. His apartment felt empty, even though Mitch had stayed for an hour, watching a ball game and drinking beer. He knew his friend was just trying to keep him company during his heartbreak. Mitch had claimed Sandi had kicked him out when she'd felt inspired to paint, but he knew his friend too well to believe it. Eve was right; Mitch couldn't lie.

"I'm fine. I'm here and I don't expect any special treatment. I'd like to get back to work. I *need* to get back to work." He noticed how tense she was sitting in the chair. Her back was straight, her shoulders back, and her eyes were full of determination.

"I have no problem with you going back to work, provided you take it easy." He looked at her a little longer. She was wearing one of his favorite shirts. The red brought out the deepness of her skin and the richness of her hair. He'd always like her best in red. Her eyes looked clear and he could see that she was telling the truth—she looked like she was ready to get back to work. He started to stand back up.

"I found a diary," she said, looking down at her hands.

He leaned back on the table and crossed his arms. "Yes, we figured you would. So? Anything I should know about?" He'd dreaded this moment. Why wasn't she yelling at him yet?

"No!" She looked up and he had the pleasure of seeing her cheeks heat.

He'd thought her diary would have shed some light on the true nature of their relationship. Maybe there was something in it that even he hadn't seen coming.

"She was pretty mean to you." She looked back down at her hands. Even though they were still in her lap, he could tell she was mentally fidgeting.

"She?" He asked.

"I, well…Eve, the other Eve." She looked at him and raised and lowered her shoulders. "It's hard to explain since I don't think the same way that she did. I can't…I guess it's hard to explain," she repeated and looked back at her hands.

"I understand. She wasn't too mean. I think she enjoyed seeing me flustered." He smiled a little. "Actually, I'd like to hope that she enjoyed some of the arguments we had. I know I did."

She looked at him and smiled a little. "Yes, she said it was a step in the relationship."

His smile dropped away. "Eve, I'd like to explain about…"

She quickly stood and shook her head. "No, you don't have to. I read her diary. She had it all planned out. How she would buy into the company." She frowned and started walking towards the door. "I… I should get to work."

He quickly walked over to her and took her shoulders, waiting for her to look at him. "If you know, why do I get the feeling you're trying to avoid me? That you're avoiding talking about the one thing we need to talk about."

"I just can't deal with this right now. I've just found out who she…who I was, how I feel. I need to find out again for myself. And this time, make some pretty big decisions. For now, I'd like it if we can be friends again."

He didn't think his heart could break again but hearing those words from her caused a pain he didn't know if he'd ever recover from.

"No, I don't want to go back to square one. I know you're going through some things, but I want to be here, with you. I know who I am, how I feel about you. That's been clear for a very long time." He felt her pull against his hold. Releasing her shoulders, he watched her step back.

"Carter, I just can't right now. I have to trust before I can decide if I want to continue with anything further." She had one hand on the door and looked like she was trying to run from a fire. He'd never seen her like this before. Even after her big break up with Steve, she'd always appeared calm. Never had she acted like she was panicked. "I have to get to work."

He must have sat there looking at the closed door for a while. When Mitch walked in, he was too deep in thought to realize.

"Hello? Earth to Carter." Mitch knocked his knuckles on his forehead.

"Hmm? What do you want?" Carter walked around his desk and sat down. He didn't trust himself to stand too close to anyone at the moment. He wanted to punch someone, and right now, Mitch was being just the right amount of annoying.

"I said…Do you want to go to the movies with Sandi and I this weekend? We're seeing the new zombie movie." His friend smiled. "Sandi has never seen a zombie movie and I think it's about time she was introduced to the walking dead."

"Sure, whatever." He looked down at the stack of papers on his desk, not really hearing his friend. Paperwork had stacked up during his month hiatus. It was going to take him three months just to get back on top of everything, especially since his mind was not focused on the task. He felt like throwing it all in the trash. Taking up a folder, he tossed it across the room. When it hit the wall, he smiled.

"That bad, huh?" Mitch sat in the chair Eve had just vacated.

Carter stood up and started to pace. "She wants to be friends. Just friends. She read her diary and found out that she was the reason that number was so high on the buy-in. But that doesn't change her mind. She has to trust before she can go further with our relationship. Trust!" Carter ran his hands through his hair, wishing he could pull it out. "Trust has never been an issue between us before. She's always trusted us, ever since that event when we were kids. Why is she telling me she has to trust now?" He paced across the room, gaining speed in his steps. What he wanted was to take a run. Looking out the large window, he saw the snow falling and felt even more frustrated.

"Take it easy." Mitch stood and stopped him from pacing. "We need to look at this differently. We have to see her as a completely new person. She isn't our old Eve. We're complete strangers to her. She's a complete stranger to us."

He pushed his friend's hands off him. "No, not to me." He stormed from the room, stopping briefly at his assistant's desk and telling her he was heading to the gym and he'd be back later.

That night, he lay awake in bed. When his phone rang around midnight, he was still awake.

"Yo?"

"Carter is that you? Someone's trying to break into my apartment." Eve's voice sounded distant. Instantly he was out of bed, putting on his shoes.

"Stay where you are. I'll be right there." He grabbed a sweatshirt and rushed out the door.

Eve put a hand over her mouth, trying to hush her breathing. She watched a dark form cross in front of her hiding spot. Fear caused her to freeze. She felt pins all over her skin like she was being poked by a million needles. The shadow crossed again, and she heard a male voice cuss. Then she heard her front door slam open and Carter's voice as he called to her. She was still frozen. The person was right in front of her; if she called out, he'd find her. Then she heard Carter running towards her bedroom and closed her eyes.

What had she done? How had she ended up calling him instead of the police? What if the man had a weapon? What if Carter got shot and died? Before she knew what she was doing, she opened her closet door and flung herself at the man.

When their bodies hit, his legs hit the side of the bed and they tumbled over. She landed on his chest and started hitting him while screaming for Carter.

She realized two things at once. First, the man wasn't fighting her back. Second, Carter was laughing. She looked up and saw him standing over them, his hands on his hips as he looked down.

She glared at him, then turned to look at the man. He was gorgeous. His dark hair had been slicked back, and his eyes were a crystal blue. He had a slight dimple in his chin and from what she could tell, he was solid muscle under her. He was frowning, causing her to notice his perfect lips.

"If you're quite done, would you mind leaving us alone? We'd like to get reacquainted," he said with a rich accent.

"Oh, no you don't." Carter's voice turned dark. "You broke her heart once. Don't think we'll stand by to let it happen again." Eve looked back up at Carter and could see the humor had left his face. "Eve, you can continue pummeling him now." He crossed his arms over his chest as she pulled herself off the man.

"Would someone please tell me what's going on?" She sat on the floor, trying to stand up. Carter reached over and, putting a hand under each of her arms, lifted her with ease.

"Well, you've just met your ex-fiancé. The man who

left you at the altar, literally." Carter tried to keep a protective arm around her shoulders, but she pushed him away.

"I don't have an ex-fiancé." She crossed her arms.

"Yes," the man said as he pulled himself off the floor, "you do. Me, Steve Hopper. We were engaged for eight years, three months and four days."

"Eight years?" She leaned against her dresser. "Why would I be engaged for eight years?"

"Exactly!" Carter smiled and leaned next to her. "We wondered the same thing. Well, when he finally got around to telling us why it took so long to put a ring on it, we were all surprised. It seems that Steve here has a wife and child in California. You were just his East Coast fling. Not a bad deal. He had free rent, all the attention he could get without a lasting commitment, and you." Carter frowned.

She glared at him. "I didn't read about him in my diary." She nodded toward Steve, who was sitting on the edge of the bed. "Get off that." She waved him away. She couldn't explain it, but she didn't want him near her bed. He stood and frowned.

"Oh, right. You burned our last one." He smiled a little and she felt shivers running down her spine.

"Why are you here?" She stood in front of him and pointed at his chest. "Is it true? Were you trying to waltz in here and start something new? How did you get in?" She gasped. "Do you have a key?" She searched his pockets and found a ring of keys.

He tried to grab them, but she slapped his hands away. She searched the ring and when she found one that looked like hers, she rushed to the front door, checking it. It fit perfectly. It took some doing, but she removed the key from the ring and put it in her robe pocket, then she tossed his keys out her front door.

Carter and Steve had followed her out of the bedroom, Carter following Steve closely, a frown on his face.

"Hey!" Steve yelled as he rushed after his keys. When he stepped outside the door, she called after him, "Don't ever come back." Then she slammed the door behind him and flipped the dead bolted.

Leaning back against the door, she jolted as she felt him kick the door.

"Don't be childish, Eve. Let me explain," he called out through the door. "Kim and I are divorced. I made it final just last month. I couldn't live without you, baby. Please, just open this door and we can talk about it."

Eve closed her eyes and leaned back on the door again. "Was I a gullible person?"

"No," Carter said. When she opened her eyes, he was standing close. Steve was still trying to convince her to open the door, but his voice faded away as she looked into Carter's eyes. "You were the strongest, most honest, and least patient person I've ever known." He smiled a little as his hand reached up and brushed a strand of hair away from her forehead. "I never thought he was right for you." He leaned a little closer to her and she realized she was out of breath.

"Carter…" she started, but then he was kissing her, and she forgot about Steve on the other side of the door. Forgot about the contract, about not trusting herself after what she'd read in her diary. Forgot everything but the feeling of him next to her, of his hands on her.

When he started pulling her back towards her bedroom, her mind cleared.

"No." She pulled away. "I can't." She pulled her robe closed. "Please, Carter. I just can't." She walked into her living room and looked out the windows at the dark city. "I didn't even know I had been engaged let alone for eight years." She turned and motioned towards the front door. Steve had either gone quiet or had left. Either way, she didn't care. "I thought I would be okay with just being, but I need to know more. Seeing my parents, seeing the contract…What kind of person was I? I'm so thankful for my two best friends, really, I am, but there was a side of me even you guys didn't know. I need to be okay with it. To find out if she's still here."

He nodded. "I know. Mitch talked to me. I know you need time. I'm sorry I pressured you." He started to back up.

"Carter?" She waited until he turned. "How did I call you?" She looked down at the phone in her robe pocket, she could have sworn she'd hit the contact that said, "Emergency" on it. Then she looked up at him and frowned. "How did you get here so quickly?"

He smiled. "I live on the twenty-fifth floor. I'm the one that told you about the opening in the building. I'm always the one you call for emergencies. Like when your sink stopped up last year." He smiled. "I'll make sure he's gone and tell building security not to allow him in again. Night, Eve." He walked to the door and closed it quietly behind him.

CHAPTER 15

Christmas was quickly approaching. Eve found a pattern at work and settled into it and actually started enjoying her job. Carter was right, it wasn't a hard job, just tiring. She felt like she was fake with most of their clients. She smiled and stroked their egos as she assured them they were the best at what they did. Almost every one of them fell for it. There were only a few that she just didn't know how to handle, so she ended up bringing Mitch or Carter along during the meetings.

They had a holiday party at the office and she found she really enjoyed a lot of the other employees. She tried avoiding Carter when she could, but on several occasions, she'd seen heat seep into his eyes and knew it matched hers.

Every night she'd fallen asleep reading her many diaries. She'd found a box of them tucked away in the top shelf of her closet.

How had Mitch and Carter not known she had a wicked side? She'd known for years that Carter had a thing for her. She'd exploited it to her personal gain. She even went as far as wearing outfits she knew he particularly liked when she needed him to give her something.

She had started believing she was no better than her parents, after all. From what she'd seen, Carter and Mitch were two of the most honest people she'd ever met. Her diaries were full of kind acts from them, dating back to when she was in college.

She'd found the part where she had met Steve at a party on campus. She'd been so dazzled by his looks, everything else had fallen to the side. She'd even known Carter and Mitch didn't approve of him, but she didn't care. She'd wanted him, and after learning more about the other Eve, she knew she always got what she wanted.

The last thing the other Eve had had her eyes on was Carter. All the more reason for her to assess her feelings for him now. Was it evil Eve after him, or was she really falling for him herself?

She was at the Christmas party, standing in the small crowded room filled with all the K&E employees when she felt a familiar pull. Knowing he was looking at her, she turned and met his eyes.

He looked especially handsome tonight. The first day back at the office, she'd been shocked at how good he looked in a suit. Their entire time in Maine he'd been wearing jeans and shirts. Sexy attire for sure, but now, he was dressed up and looking even sexier.

"Merry Christmas." He held out a flat box, with a smile on his face. "Mitch wanted to be here when I did this…"—he looked around— "but I think Sandi and he are in some dark corner, making out." He smiled and so did she.

"They are so cute when they do that, aren't they?" She said.

"Cute?" He chuckled, "I wouldn't describe it as cute."

She reached up and took the box from him. "I'm beginning to find out that I like surprises." She started opening the box slowly. "And apparently that I like to open my presents very slowly." She laughed.

"Yes, it was always very annoying." He tried to reach over and rip off the paper for her. She slapped his hands away playfully.

Finally, when she lifted the lid, she noticed a bundle of papers. Frowning, she lifted them from the tissue paper and set the box down on a table behind her.

"What's this?" She started reading the bold print.

"It's a new contract, splitting the company into thirds. It's been long overdue. All you need to do is sign." He handed her a pen just as Mitch and Sandi walked out of his office, smiling.

"Oh, you've given it to her?" They rushed over, smiling even bigger.

"Well?" Mitch looked between them. "Is she okay with the new price?"

"New?" She looked down at the paperwork and found the spot where the buy-in number was. Her chin dropped. "You can't do this." She pushed the paperwork back at the trio. "I won't sign it. I shouldn't be given a third of this company."

Mitch sighed. "Listen, Eve. You may not remember this, but we've been all over the spectrum. From the largest amount you wanted to this." He handed her back the paperwork. "Each time we present you with these, you aren't happy with something. It's almost as if you don't want to become partner." Mitch looked to Carter. She noticed then that Carter's shoulders had sunk.

"We thought this was the right thing to do, considering the situation," Mitch said.

"It is a very generous offer; I just don't deserve a third of this company. Not now." She looked between everyone. "I don't feel like what I'm doing is worth it."

Carter and Mitch laughed. "Is that all? When we signed you on, we were sinking. The business was about to go under due to over-commitment and a dive in the economy. But in the last few years, you've revived it. You're the reason we're in the position we are today. You've more than earned it. You deserve it." He put the paperwork back into her hands. "Sign it, Eve. Trust your two best friends, at least in this area."

She saw a flash in Carter's eyes. Reaching up, she took the pen he held out towards her. Turning around, she signed her name on the line. When she turned back around, the entire office cheered and tossed confetti at her. Champagne was passed out, and she was congratulated more times than she could remember. Someone turned on some music, and the party got even rowdier.

The noise level mixed with the champagne caused her head to start aching, so she slipped into her office to try and get some quiet time. She'd read all about her plans for K&E. How she'd get the two of them to let her buy-in, then she'd take the business to the top, earning more money and basically running the company and her friends, since she knew their weaknesses and how to get what she wanted.

Loosening her hair from the braid she'd worn, she walked over to her window and leaned her head against the cool glass. She wished she could just come clean to her friends, but every time she tried to talk to them about how she was in the past, they'd just laugh at her and smile. Then they'd say something like, *"Yup, good old Eve,"* like they were pacifying her. It was driving her crazy.

Now she had gotten everything the old Eve had wanted. Hearing the door click shut, she turned and looked at Carter. Well, she thought, almost everything.

"Hi, is your head hurting you?" He walked towards her, concern on his face. His voice was so soothing. It had been the one steady thing in the last few months. Hearing him always made her feel safe. She felt her throat close up, so she just nodded.

"Do you want me to take you home?" An image of them naked in her bed flashed so quickly in her mind, she grabbed the side of her desk. Shaking her head, no, she tried to breathe through the desire.

He continued to walk towards her, slowly. "You didn't have to sign the contract, you know." He stopped right before her, then took her hand in his and raised it to his lips.

She watched in amazement as he kissed her fingers, then twisted her hand so he could place a soft kiss on the inside of her palm.

"I know." It was no more than a whisper. "I wanted to." She watched his eyelashes as he focused on her wrist.

"You look lovely tonight. Have I mentioned this is my favorite color on you?" He traced the neckline of her dress, causing her to hold her breath. The little red number had called out to her when she'd been getting ready for the party. The dress and the spiky red heels were a killer combination.

She shook her head. "I read it in my diary." She gasped as his finger dipped along the line, just above her nipples. She felt them harden and heard him groan when he noticed them poking through the light material.

"So, you wore this just for me tonight?" He leaned down and placed a soft kiss on her neck. She tilted her head, giving him better access as she enjoyed the softness of his lips, the heat of his mouth on her skin.

"Yes. No. I can't think." She gripped his arms trying to steady herself.

"Good, let's not think for a while." He rained kisses along the neckline of her low-cut dress. When he reached the sensitive spot above her heart, his tongue darted out and licked his way back to her ear. "I want you so badly. I've missed you in my bed. I've missed falling asleep with you, waking up next to you, being inside you." He kissed her lips and she moaned as he pulled her close to him. She felt his desire press up against her stomach and reached over to slowly rub him. He moaned as his hands started to run over her. "Eve, I don't think—"

"I thought you said not to think." She reached for his zipper. "I've missed you, too. I want you so badly. Please, Carter."

He was kissing her again, pulling her up onto the corner of her desk. Her dress hiked up as his hands ran over her hips, over her sides. Then one of his hands moved under her skirt, spreading her legs wide so he could stand between them.

"Now, please," she moaned and leaned her head back as he kissed her neck. He pushed her farther onto her desk, knocking several items off the edge. In one quick motion, he removed her silk panties and was inside her as she cried his name and held on.

What had he done? His face was buried in her hair. He was still buried in her and even felt himself getting harder thinking about how good she felt. Stop it, he ordered himself. She'd asked for time and he'd locked them in her office and taken her on her desk. Sure, she'd pretty much seduced him into it, but that didn't make it any better. She'd asked for time. Did this mean she'd made her decision?

"Eve?" He rose up above her, looking down at her smiling face. Her hair was fanned out on the dark wood. Her dress was hiked up past her hips and her chest was freed from the plunging neckline that had driven him crazy all night. He wanted to lean down and suck on her perfect nipples, but he needed to straighten a few things out first. "Does this mean you've taken enough time?"

Her smile fell away, and she slowly shook her head. She tried to sit up, but he held her still. "Carter, let me up."

"No," he shook his head. "Not yet. I want to hear your reasons while you're exposed. While I'm still inside you, while you're still breathless from desire. I want to hear why we can't be together."

She closed her eyes and leaned her head back against the desk. "I'm a mean person. I've done things. I've manipulated you and Mitch to get what I've wanted. I'm not a good person, Carter." She opened her eyes and raised her hands to his face. "You deserve a nice person. You deserve someone better."

He smiled and laughed. "No, Eve. I'm not perfect

either. I've done and said things, too." He leaned down and placed a kiss on her forehead, then pulled away. Turning away, he thought of the night he'd left her alone in the dark street. Of all the blood. Seeing her lying on the cold street. It had been all his fault. Closing his eyes on a wave of pain, he tried to block the memory of it from his mind.

She touched his shoulder, jogging him from the memories. Turning, he tried to smile. "I'm sorry if I overstepped it here." He motioned to her desk. He knew he'd never be able to see it again without thinking of her spread out over it.

"No, it was my fault, really." She reached up and placed a kiss on his cheek. "Give me just a little more time. I'm remembering more and more each day. I want to make sure what we have is what is best for us both."

He shook his head. "I don't understand it, but if you want more time, I'll try to give it to you." He held out his arm for her to take. "Now, do you think we can rejoin the party without anyone realizing we just had some of the hottest sex this office has ever witnessed on your desk?" He smiled, and she laughed.

When they opened the door, they realized they could have walked out naked and no one would have noticed. The lights were flashing and there was an actual Congo line going around the entire office.

"Oh, this reminds me." He turned her towards him, so she could hear over the loud music. "What do you say to going with me to Mitch and Sandi's New Year's Eve party?"

He could tell she thought about it for a second, then nodded her head. "Sounds great." She laughed as she was pulled into the middle of the dance line and whisked away.

CHAPTER 16

Over the next few days, Eve tried to keep her mind on her work. She'd taken on more clients since she was feeling more confident in her job and in her position at K&E. Carter and Mitch kept trying to tell her to take it slow, but she had a fire under her since signing the contract. Three days after the Christmas party, she walked out of her office to ask Lesley something when she overheard the woman talking on the phone.

"I'm sorry, Miss Taylor isn't available right now, but if you'd like I can patch you through to Mr. Edwards again."

"Lesley," Eve interrupted.

"Please hold." Lesley put the call on hold and Eve could see the fear cross her eyes. "Yes, Miss Taylor?"

"Who's calling and why am I unavailable?" She walked over to the front of her desk, not knowing the move was meant to intimidate the younger woman.

"I'm sorry, Miss Taylor. I was under orders by Mr. Edwards. It's Mr. Thomas, the head of the Thomas Ad agency in Chicago. If you would like, I can patch the call to you now." Lesley's eyes darted towards Carter's office, then back at Eve.

Eve crossed her arms and thought of a dozen ways to kill Carter Edwards. "Yes, do that." She turned to go. "Oh, and Lesley, from now on, I'll be taking *all* of my calls."

Walking into her office, she punched the button to answer the call. "Eve Taylor."

"Eve, dear. I've been so worried about you. It seems no one at your office wants to patch me through. I had thought about coming down there myself to see if you were all right."

"I can assure you, Mr. Thomas, that I am doing very well. Thank you for asking."

"Mr. Thomas? Are we not on a first name basis now?" There was something in his voice that Eve just couldn't pinpoint.

"I'm sorry, I can't seem to remember your first name. I'm not sure if anyone has mentioned, but a few months back I lost my memory."

He chuckled. "Yes, I did hear about your nasty fall. Simon, you used to call me Simon." His voice turned deep and husky sounding. "At least every time you came up to Chicago and stayed with me."

Eve felt flustered. Here she was on the phone with an ex-lover and she hadn't even known about it. The name Simon Thomas hadn't appeared anywhere in any of her diaries. And she'd read all the way back to her college days at this point.

"I'm sorry, Simon. I do hope you understand." She said.

"Yes," he chuckled again. "I fully understand."

Ten minutes later Eve marched into Carter's office and

slammed his door behind her. He was on the phone and looked up. When he saw her face, he apologized to whomever he was talking to and made a quick excuse and hung up.

"How did your conversation with Simon Thomas go?" He leaned back in his chair and smiled a little.

"So," Eve looked towards his door and thought of firing Lesley. "She tattles as well as obeys your every order."

"Oh now"—he got up and walked to lean on the front of his desk— "don't take it out on Lesley. We were just concerned that you were taking on too much. Actually, if you want to be mad at someone, talk to Mitchell. He was the one that suggested we screen your calls and mail."

Eve started pacing in front of his desk. "It's you I'm mad at." She turned on him. "Why didn't you tell me I'd been offered full partnership at Thomas Ad Agency?" She pointed a finger into his chest. "Were you afraid I'd get a better offer and leave? Or did you just want to tie me into a contract here?"

She watched his face pale. "Eve, I had no idea Simon had offered you a partnership. The night we arrived in Chicago you told me you had a dinner scheduled with him. But when we agreed on our contract, you canceled with him." Carter stood and took her shoulders. "Honest."

She looked up into his eyes and could tell he was telling the truth. Her shoulders relaxed a little and most of the steam she'd built up in the last few minutes died away.

"Well," she didn't know what to say, mostly because he was looking at her with softened eyes. "I suppose I can see why you wouldn't have known." She thought of her diaries and how the old Eve had planned to get what she wanted out of K&E. Maybe she used Simon Thomas to get the contract she wanted. She straightened her shoulders a little. "I guess it all turned out for the best. I mean, I hadn't even mentioned my professional relationship with Simon, let alone my personal relationship with him, in my diaries. Why would I want to tie myself to him as a partner?" Carter's hands tightened on her shoulders and anger crossed his eyes. She didn't know what she'd said, but she could almost see steam rolling off him.

"What?" he said between his teeth.

"My diaries," she whispered, trying to think of why it mattered to Carter who she'd been within her past. They'd talked about some of her past relationships shortly after Steve had surprised her in her apartment. He'd listed a few other men she'd dated, but none of them had been named Simon. "My diaries hadn't mentioned that Simon and I had been an item. But he seemed to think we'd been an item every time I traveled to Chicago."

"He's lying." Carter dropped his hands and marched from the room. She quickly followed him into Mitch's office. Mitch looked up from a stack of paperwork.

"Tell her that she's never, would never, have been with Simon Thomas." Carter pointed towards her. She stood just inside Mitch's door, which she quietly shut behind her.

Mitch laughed. "You and Simon Thomas." Then his face dropped. "No chance in hell."

"See!" Carter turned to her. "Now, the question is, why did Simon lie to you about it. Maybe you should sit down and tell us exactly what the two of you just talked about." He pointed to a chair.

That night when she arrived back at her apartment, there were red roses sitting in front of her door. She smiled and smelled them as she walked in her door. The note attached read.

"I'm so happy you're better. – With love, Simon"

She'd listened to what Carter and Mitch had said about the man. To be honest, she didn't agree with them. The man she'd talked to on the phone had been nothing but polite and showed concern for her health. She'd even begun to wonder if what Simon had said was true. Could she have kept their relationship a secret because she didn't want Mitch, or worse, Carter to find out about it?

That night, she hunted through her diaries trying to find any hint at their relationship. There was a quick note three days before she'd left to go to her last trip to Chicago.

"Heading to windy city to w&d fb player Tom Russell. Have d plans with S. We'll see if I can use to my advantage."

She'd had a few more memory episodes since arriving back to New York. None of them had caused her to black out, but on several occasions, she'd gotten a headache and her vision had gotten a little gray. For the most part, she was starting to remember who she was. She still called this other side of her the other Eve, because she didn't always agree with the way she'd handled things. Especially when it came to her relationship with Carter. Other Eve, at least from what she could tell in her diaries, was using him to get what she wanted: physical pleasure and partnership in K&E. The fact that they were best friends hadn't even stopped her from taking what she wanted.

She thought of her relationship with him now, and how she felt. He'd told her that he loved her. Other Eve had mentioned love as well, but she thought she had meant she loved what he could give her. Eve thought about it and knew that she didn't care what Carter could give her, that she was really and truly falling for him. It both thrilled her and scared her.

The next day, Lesley patched another call through. This one she'd wished she hadn't. "Miss Taylor, your mother is on the line."

Eve took a deep breath before she picked up the phone. "Hello?"

"Hello, dear. I just wanted to let you know that we're having our annual New Years' party. I know you never show up, but like every year, I call and invite you."

"Thank you, but I've already made other plans." She said.

"I understand. Besides, it's probably for the best since your father doesn't know that I call each year. I just wanted you to know that you're always welcome here." She could hear her mother's voice hitch. "Eve, I wanted you to know that I'm very happy you've made partner. Carter called and told us. I know I don't say it often, but I'm very proud of you."

She couldn't explain it, but her heart jumped out of her chest and tears started running down her face. At that moment, she knew without a doubt that it was the first time her mother had ever said those words to her. And she didn't need a box load of diaries to tell her it was true.

The night of New Year's came and when Carter showed up at Eve's door to get her, he was totally shocked to see the little number she was wearing. It was a simple yet sexy black dress with a plunging neckline that crisscrossed over her chest. The tall black boots went all the way up her calf and stopped just below her knees. Three-inch spikes made her almost as tall as he was, allowing him to look directly into her eyes. He held out the bundle of flowers he'd brought her without saying a word.

"Thank you." She took her time smelling them and burying her face in the soft petals. "Would you like to come in?" She moved back to allow him to walk in.

He walked past her, his eyes never leaving her. When she closed the door and turned to smile at him, he said, "You look beautiful." She smiled even more.

"Thank you. I've just discovered a new hobby of mine and whipped this together last week." She turned and showed off the dress. His eyes traveled over the slim lines of her body. The cut of the dress showed off her curves, making him want to run his hands all over her. Then his mind cleared.

"You? You made this?" The shock must have shown on his face because she laughed.

"Yes, along with a few other things. I didn't know if the talent had survived the head bump, but by the look on your face, I'd say it did." She walked over and began putting the flowers into a vase and then she set them by a large bundle of red roses.

"Where did you get those?" He asked.

"Oh, aren't they nice? Simon sent those the other day." She smelled his flowers again and turned to Carter. He tried to wipe the anger from his eyes before she noticed it. Apparently, he hadn't succeeded.

"Don't be like that. For now, I'm just enjoying the smell and look of them. Besides, he's clear in Chicago and"—she walked slowly towards him and he quickly forgot about Simon Thomas— "you're here with me." She walked right into his arms and kissed him and he forgot about everything but the feel of her against him.

When they arrived at the party in the large lobby of one of Mitch's favorite local restaurants a half hour later, he was still so wound up, he was finding it hard to concentrate on talking to his friends. His eyes kept darting towards Eve as she talked to Sandi across the crowded ballroom. He tried to spend as much time by her side as he could, but with the crowd, he'd lost sight of her on several occasions.

He'd been talking to a good friend, Trent, the owner and head chef of Manhattan Nights, the restaurant where the party was being held. Trent had been a roommate of Mitch's during college, and they'd all remained good friends since then. Trent's success was the stuff legends were made of, at least when it came to the restaurant business. His place was always packed, and most people had to wait weeks to get a table booked, but for them, Trent always had an empty table. Actually, it was a standard that if they had a party or event, they held it here. To return the favor, K&E handled all Trent's advertising needs. It was a mutual benefit and served them both well.

It was shortly before midnight when Carter started hunting the crowd for Eve. He wanted to make sure he rang in the New Year right. He spotted Mitch and Sandi sitting in a dark booth and walked over towards them.

"Have either of you seen Eve?" His eyes were still scanning the room.

"She said she needed some air. She just stepped out." Sandi smiled and pointed towards the large glass doors that lead out to a patio.

"Thanks. Oh, happy New Year," he said as he walked away.

When he walked out onto the patio, he saw several couples strolling around the small, covered patio. The wind was cold enough that he pulled his dress jacket closed. Eve was out here in this? What was she thinking?

He scanned the dark pathways and was about to turn back into the room when he saw her running out of the back gate across the courtyard. He saw a man dressed in black right behind her. Carter didn't hesitate; he took off at full speed.

$\mathcal{E}$ve was enjoying the party. Even though the loudness of the crowd and music had caused a small headache to start, she still smiled and chatted with everyone she knew. She'd been introduced to a few friends she hadn't remembered. They had all introduced themselves and told her how they knew each other. She was sitting in a booth with Mitch and Sandi, watching Carter work his magic on a few clients. She enjoyed watching how smooth he was with everyone. He looked like he was enjoying himself. The dim lights and the mix of a new song that had just come on made her head pound even more. Excusing herself, she made her way across the floor towards the glass doors and cool air. She'd hoped for some quiet, but when she stepped out the door, the music was still loud enough that she continued walking in the cold until the light and sound disappeared, leaving just the cold breeze and the dim lights of the city. She stopped and took a deep breath as she wrapped her arms around herself. She didn't feel the cold, didn't notice as she shivered. All that mattered was that the music was dull and the lights were low. Taking another deep breath to steady herself, she almost choked on the rich, musky scent of someone's cologne. Instantly, her mind whirled to another place, to another time, much like this one.

"Hello, Eve." He stood shadowed in darkness. Her arm hurt from where he'd pulled her from the sidewalk into the alley. She rubbed her wrist and straightened her shoulders.

"What do you want?" She wasn't too steady on her feet; after all, two green beers had caused her head to swim. But she still understood the situation she was in and tried to edge her way towards the mouth of the alley.

"I'm very disappointed with your behavior. First, you cancel our dinner plans and now I hear from Mitchell that you're signing on as partner with K&E."

"Really, Simon, what I do is none of your business." She turned to leave, but he grabbed her wrist again, causing her to let out a small squeal. When he started to twist it, she looked into his eyes. Anger filled his face and she watched as his hands began to shake.

"We had an agreement," he pulled her close and the smell of his cologne almost gagged her. She tried to pull away, to push him back, but he just pulled her closer. "We were going to go places, be together." He leaned down and plastered his mouth over hers. She kicked and pushed him away, and when she'd finally freed her mouth and arm, she slapped him across the face.

He pulled back and laughed, twisting her arm painfully around her back. "I will have you, both as a partner and in my bed. I know your type. All you need is a firm hand. You'll see." He started pulling her towards the end of the alleyway. "I've got a suite at the Drake. We'll just head over there and make our future arrangements."

She thought about her plans with Carter, about her future with him and with K&E. Everything, all of her malicious plans to take K&E to another level disappeared. The only thing remained was Carter's voice, his face, the feel of his hands on her. There was no way she would let Simon touch her like that. No way she'd ever be partners with him.

Kicking out, she hit his shin hard enough that he released her. Then she screamed as his hand swiped out to backhand her. She watched him smile as she lost her footing and fell backward. When her head hit the cold cement, blackness engulfed her. The last thought she had was of Carter. Of never seeing him again.

She jerked to reality. Her head spun, and her vision was going gray. The smell of Simon's cologne was stronger, and she knew he was close. Looking around, she could only see darkness. Rushing towards what she thought was the party, she prayed she was heading in the right direction. When she ran into a small gate, she realized she'd gotten turned around. Now she was in the back alley of the hotel, probably where employees took their smoke breaks. Shaking her head, trying to clear her vision, she realized for the first time that she was freezing.

She saw a large light and started to head towards it, only to have her arm yanked behind her as she was being pushed up against a brick wall.

"I wondered if you'd remembered me, yet." Simon's face hovered near hers, the smell of his cologne gagging her. "Imagine my surprise when I found out that you'd lost your memory. Here was my second chance. I tried to find you after the incident, but you'd disappeared. Then I heard that you'd disappeared to Maine and found you hiding out in that place. I watched you and Carter for a while, trying to find the right time to get close, but then you left. I came here tonight to try and convince you, but when I saw you take off, I knew you'd remembered. What you don't remember is that you enjoyed my rough hands. Trip after trip to Chicago, you'd beg me." He smiled, and she felt like clawing his eyes out, but her hands were now trapped behind her and the wall. "We were lovers, Eve. You had a dark side no one knew about, only me." He leaned in to kiss her, but instead he was ripped from her. She spun around and started to fall, only to be steadied. Her eyesight still hadn't returned, but the feel of Carter's arms around her assured her she was safe.

"Edwards! This is the last time you'll come between me and Eve." Carter pushed her gently behind him.

"Simon, you're delusional. You've always had a twisted mind." Carter said.

She heard someone growl, then Carter disappeared from her grasp. In the darkness of the alley, she could only make out two dark forms as they battled. She could hear the blows and grunts as fists connected. Should she run for help? Where would she go? Looking around, everything was dark except for a few lights. Which direction? Her head was pounding, and her vision was so bad now, she couldn't make out who was who.

"Stop! Someone help!" she screamed down the alley. She moved forward only to be shoved back, her arm twisted behind her.

"Don't! Move and I'll kill her." She felt something near

her neck. Then Carter's face came into view. His mouth was bleeding and one of his eyes was half shut.

"Touch her and die." Carter swiped at the blood on his mouth. His dinner jacket was ripped, and his white shirt had blood spots on the front.

"You've always been a pain in my ass," Simon growled. "Back in college you always got what I wanted first." He looked between them and smirked. "Well, this is one time you won't end up with the prize."

Then Eve felt a sharp burst of heat in her side. Simon threw her towards Carter and she landed softly in his arms. He started to scream for help as Simon ran out of the dark alley.

Looking up, she realized she was on the cold ground. Carter's face hovered above hers as he talked to her. She couldn't hear his voice, she desperately wanted to hear his voice.

Reaching up with a shaky hand, she touched his face and smiled. "Shhh, it's okay. I meant to tell you... I planned to tell you at midnight. I love you." The darkness was coming too fast, she had more she wanted to say, but her teeth were chattering now, and her vision had completely gone. Her hearing returned right before the darkness consumed her.

"Don't leave me, Eve. Don't you dare leave me."

Carter paced the hallway outside the waiting room. There were too many people crammed in the small space for his liking. This way, he could see the doctor first. Mitch and

Sandi sat on a bench outside the doors, watching him. Sandi's eyes were red and puffy from crying.

Two hours later, Eve's parents strolled in like they had all the time in the world. He could see the concern on her mother's face, but her father showed no emotion.

Mitch stood and greeted them. Carter tried not to acknowledge them as they went into the waiting area to wait with the rest of the party.

Two times, two times he'd seen Eve lying on the cold ground in an alley. There was no way he'd allow it to happen again. Stupid. He'd been so stupid to take his eyes off her. Why hadn't he guessed it had been Simon who'd attacked her the first time?

He'd been interviewed by the police, just like the first time. However, this time, he had a name to give them. When Mitch had found out it was Simon, his friend's face had filled with anger.

"Son of a…" he stopped and looked towards Sandi. "I bet we can tie those threatening letters back to him as well. I should have seen it." Mitch had pulled Sandi close as she'd cried. Then Sandi had demanded to take a look at Carter's bloody lip and a black eye. He hadn't even felt the pain.

Three hours after they'd wheeled Eve upstairs for surgery, the doctor walked into the hallway outside the surgery waiting area.

"Are you family?" He asked Carter and Mitch.

"Yes, I'm her brother and this is her fiancé," Mitch piped in, winking at Carter.

"Very well. Eve's very lucky. The cut pierced her liver and nicked her gallbladder, but we've repaired most of the damage. She does have a slight crack in her ninth or false rib, but she's out of rough water. We're moving her to ICU where we'll want her to stay until she regains consciousness. I've read her charts and with the recent head injuries, I'll want to keep her for a few extra days, just to make sure."

Carter turned around when the waiting room door opened, and Eve's parents walked out. They introduced themselves to the doctor.

"I was just telling your daughter's fiancé, here, that we'll be moving Eve to the ICU. If you want, you can head up there. Only one visitor at a time is allowed in the room, but I see no reason why you can't see her once they get her settled."

Eve's father glared at Carter and her mother smiled slightly. When the doctor was gone, her father turned to him. "Fiancé?"

"Yes, sir. Is there a problem?" He held his shoulders back, ready for a fight.

"No. It's about damn time, don't you think?" The older man said, then grabbed his wife's arm and started walking towards the elevators.

Mitch slapped him on the back. "Well, I guess congratulations are in order." He laughed. "I guess I'll just pop in there and tell everyone else the good news. Why don't you head up and see about seeing our girl?"

It took Eve almost a day to regain consciousness. Her eyes fluttered opened and the first thing she said was his name. He was right there, touching her hand and talking to her. When she asked about Simon, he told her the truth.

"By the time the police arrived at his hotel, he'd already checked out. So far, he hasn't checked back in with his secretary, and she doesn't know where he's gone.

Yesterday they found his private jet on an abandoned airstrip just outside of Phoenix. The police think he's crossed the border." He frowned. If he ever saw the man again, he'd kill him, and he knew Mitch felt the same way.

"Your parents are here." He smiled at her. "I have to say, I'm surprised they've stuck around this long. But they wanted to make sure you were okay."

"Really?" She tried to sit up a little.

"No." He tried to stop her. "Stay still."

She closed her eyes on the pain. "How bad?" she asked as she reached over and rubbed the bandages over her wound.

He shook his head. "He sliced up your liver pretty bad, nicked your gallbladder in the process. But the doc says it's your ribs that will give you problems."

He took her hand up to his mouth and kissed it. "I almost lost you again." He leaned his head down to hers and kissed her forehead. She reached up and ran her hands through his hair.

"You scared me." She said.

He pulled back and looked down at her and asked, "I scared you?"

She nodded her head, her eyes closed. "Yes, I thought he was going to kill you." She opened her eyes and he watched tears fall down her face. "I couldn't stand it if you weren't here." Her voice hitched as she took his hand and placed a soft kiss on his cut knuckles. "I love you. I don't want to live without you. I want us to live in our big house in Maine, take long walks on the beach, and have a family together."

He smiled. "I'd like that as well." Then he kissed her lips and knew everything was going to be all right.

Eve walked onto the beach, the light material of her dress blowing in the cool breeze. She could smell the flowers in her hair and hands, as well as the salt water of the ocean spray. There were three dozen chairs spread out along the water's edge. Carter and Mitch stood at the makeshift altar, which was covered in white flowers. She smiled at Carter and walked towards the pair. One of them she thought of as a brother, the other was soon to be her husband.

When she arrived at the altar, she stood off to the side and watched Sandi walk towards Carter and Mitch, and the crowd stood. Eve had outdone herself when she'd created her friend's wedding dress. The off-white silk clung and flowed in a unique design of Eastern mixed with Western cultures.

Sandi's mother smiled as she stood in the front row. Eve knew that Sandi had insisted on a traditional Western marriage, much to her mother's disapproval. But they had compromised and later next week, Eve would be a brides-maid in their second, Eastern-style wedding.

Seeing Mitch's face as his bride joined him made her smile and a tear escaped her eyes. Looking over, she smiled at Carter, who was smiling back at her.

After the wedding, when the crowd had gathered on the dance floor and around the food on the large deck over-looking the setting sun, Carter approached her and took her hand.

"How about a walk on the beach?"

"I'd love one." She smiled as he grabbed two flutes of champagne as they walked by a waiter. She no longer feared that Simon would jump from the shadows; he was rotting in a cell in Arizona. At least for the next few years, and after that…well, she had Carter to protect her from anything that might come up after that.

Carter waited until they were far enough away from the crowd before handing her the glasses. Then, smoothly, he got down on one knee and pulled a small black box from his coat pocket.

"I wanted to make this official." He smiled at her. "Eve Taylor, would you do me the honor of becoming my wife?"

She smiled down at him. "Yes, of course." She handed him his glass and took the ring and placed it on her finger. She'd seen his grandmother's ring before, in a memory. But seeing it on her own finger, shining in the dying sunlight, it was more impressive and beautiful then she remembered.

Carter stood and held up his glass. "To new beginnings and to our future." They clicked their glasses together, then drank. Then Carter pulled her into a hug and kissed her as the sun slipped below the water's edge.

If you've enjoyed this book, please consider leaving a review where you purchased it. Thanks! --Jill

PROLOGUE

Trenton walked into the old building on Fiftieth Street. He'd been looking at the old brick place for a while—staring at it, actually—since it was adjacent to his new loft. He'd had his real estate agent searching for a building all over Manhattan, but so far, she'd come up with nothing he liked. Then last week, the tenants of the place next door, an old furniture store, moved out. The place had sat empty since then.

He'd had Jessica, his agent, check on it, but the place hadn't come on the market yet. Just a few hours ago, though, he'd watched the owner, a small Korean woman, place a "for rent" sign in the large front window. He'd texted his agent and rushed down the stairs and out the door quickly.

When he'd first approached the owner, he'd been breathing hard and her eyes had gone wide like she thought she was about to be mugged. After he'd caught his breath, he'd grabbed the sign and told her what he wanted.

Now, over a month later, he looked around the building

—his building—and thought of all the work that needed to be done. He had building permits locked in his briefcase, along with bids from various reputable construction companies. He also had almost a hundred applicants to interview and train after the kitchens were completed and all his new equipment was delivered and set up. He had the bar staff to hire, stock to order, and tables and tablecloths to order. He didn't skimp on any of the details.

Smiling, he could just imagine how it would look a year from now. Manhattan Nights was going to be his first crown jewel. The doorway that would open up other doorways, and he would oversee every part of it himself, adding his touch wherever he could.

CHAPTER 1

ive years later…

Marina was running late. She looked down at the small paper in her hand and craned her neck in all directions looking for the right place. She loved her job, but she hated deadlines. And her shoes. She looked down at the new silver heels and wondered why she'd bought them in the first place.

As she quickly started walking towards her destination, she caught her reflection in a store window and remembered why she'd paid almost a hundred dollars for the pumps. They made her feet and legs look sexy. Smiling, she picked up her pace.

Two and a half blocks later, she found the spot. This place wasn't the style she usually dealt with. It was actually one of the better-known places she'd gotten a call for. Standing out front on the sidewalk, she looked up at the beautiful brick building and the black awnings with simple lettering hung that over the doors and windows. She wondered why Reggie, her boss, had wanted her to come to check out this place.

Running a hand down her skirt, she straightened her shoulders and walked towards the large glass doors. When she walked in, cool air hit her face. She took a deep breath and enjoyed it for just a moment. It was another hot summer day, but since she was wearing light clothing, the five-block hike hadn't bothered her too much.

She walked up and gave her name to the maître d'. As he was seating her, she looked around. The wait staff was well dressed in classy black and white. The tablecloths were a nice rich cream. Actually, the entire room was gorgeous. Nothing looked out of place. From the elegant artwork to the beautiful chandeliers, the place screamed class and comfort.

As she sat down, the maître d' handed her a menu and explained the specials for the day. She nodded and ordered the soup, then the maître d' left her to look over her menu. It was her job to know food. Good food. She'd been writing for the Times for over three years now and had, in that time, stepped on a lot of toes. She'd also advanced a lot of restaurants to stardom. Of course, it was all under her pen name. The only two people who knew her real identity were Reggie and Carol down in payroll.

Smiling as the waiter walked over to take her order, she mentally checked off the list of items she would note on. So far, the place was looking to be a great review.

Half an hour later, her food was delivered, and she quickly changed her mind. She ate quickly and left. She frowned the entire way home, wishing she had never stepped foot in Manhattan Nights.

Trent stared down at his morning paper and started choking on his coffee. When he recovered, he threw the rest of the paper down and marched out of his loft. Less than five minutes later, he stood in front of his staff and tried not to yell.

"Who is responsible for this?" He shook the paper. It was a quarter past one, so he knew some of his staff would have already read the review.

Angie, his sous chef, quickly looked away, so he knew she'd already seen the piece. Rob, his chef de partie, looked down at his feet. Half of the other staff refused to look him in the eye.

"I want to know who was on staff and what was served, immediately." His voice broke as he tried not to scream.

Steven, his other head chef, rushed out to get him the answers. For the last few months, Trent had left Steven in charge, so he could focus his time on the grand opening of Manhattan Nights' second location, just off of Fifth Avenue.

He stood there and waited for an explanation, thinking that obviously, he'd hired the wrong people to control his kitchen. He'd just have to step back into that role himself again until he could find someone else to take over.

He'd already hired staff for the new location, which was set to open in just under three months. But this review

—he looked down at the paper and felt his stomach roll— might set that back.

Steven rushed towards him, his face red, as he held out the schedule. Trent walked into his office and Steven followed him, close on his heels.

"Shut the door," Trent said without looking at the man. As he looked over the list of employees, he noticed that in the last week, Steven's name had been removed three times. "Did you take some time off this week?"

"Yes. I called you and left messages. My sister was sick. She needed some scans done." Trent knew that Steven's older sister was fighting cancer.

"I didn't get any messages." He looked down at his phone. "You left these on my cell?"

He shook his head no. "I left them on your home line. That's where you said to call."

Trent forwarded his home line to wherever he was so any calls should have been routed directly to him. His frown deepened. The man's answers weren't adding up. "Strange, I never received any messages." He looked over the list. "Can you tell me why M. Jensen, one of the best-known food critics in New York, would claim that our beef tartare was"—he picked up the paper and read word for word— "harder than the bottom of my shoe with less taste than my ex." He tossed the paper down in disgust.

"I'm…I'm not sure. I personally tested everything." Trent stood up and started pacing. "I know this looks bad…" Steven was fumbling with his hands and Trent could see sweat dripping down the man's face. He hated to let him go, especially now, since he'd have little time to find and hire someone else, but a review like this could break his restaurant, especially since it was from M. Jensen.

An hour and one chef later, he walked out of his office with the new schedule in hand. When he pinned it to the board, several staff members walked over and looked at it. He heard some groans, but since he was leaning up against the wall, his arms crossed, glaring at them, everyone just got back to work. Pushing away from the wall, he went and washed his hands and got to work himself. Since he was the only chef until he could find a replacement, he was working every shift until Manhattan Nights' reputation was back up to par.

That evening, they saw a huge drop in guests and over the next few weeks, the numbers continued to drop. It was quite funny how loyal customers who did nothing but praise the food and service before had decided the place was no longer good enough to frequent after reading someone else's review.

By the end of the month, the place was almost empty on weeknights. He had to do something and fast if he was going to keep his businesses afloat. And the first thing he wanted to do was track down M. Jensen and request that the man come in for another review. Or ring his neck.

First thing Monday morning, he marched into the paper and requested a meeting with one of the editors. After hitting a brick wall there, he requested another meeting with a different editor, only to be told that there was a waiting list for reviews from M. Jensen. He left an hour later, more frustrated than before.

When he walked back into the kitchen later that night he noticed that half his staff wasn't in yet. He walked over to Angie while he wrapped his apron around his hips.

"Where is everyone?" Angie had been there for him since opening day. She was the first employee he'd hired. In the last five years, he'd never seen her take a day off or heard her complain.

She looked at him and frowned. "Sick." Her blonde hair was tied back in a tight bun at the base of her head. Her blue eyes were always looking around, catching everything that went on. She was almost his height, with a stockier build, but the one thing he admired the most about her was that she knew how to cook. It was something that came naturally to her, not something she had to work at. Her organization skills were the only thing stopping Trent from moving her up. When he'd first hired her, they'd had a brief personal relationship that had become a solid working friendship.

Wiping the sweat from his brow, he realized he'd worked harder this month then he had when he'd first opened the place. Not only had he been running the kitchen and staff, he was also interviewing chefs for Steven's replacement whenever he could. So far, he had three chefs that he liked. All three would come in for a full-day interview that included them running the kitchen and staff for a complete meal.

At closing time, he walked back to his loft, totally exhausted. He still had a pile of papers to go through for the new restaurant and would no doubt be up all-night playing catch up.

When he walked in, his machine was flashing with new messages. Listening to them as he grabbed a beer, he heard his longtime friends talking about baseball season starting and groaned.

It wasn't that he didn't like baseball season—he loved

it. Unfortunately, the season started in three weeks, which meant that he'd need time free for practices and games, something he couldn't afford yet.

At least not until he'd hired a new chef, set M. Jensen straight, and earned back his reputation and customers.

This is a work of fiction. Names, characters, places, and incidents either are the product of the author's imagination or are used fictitiously, and any resemblance to actual persons, living or dead, business establishments, events or locales is entirely coincidental.

SECRET IDENTITY

DIGITAL ISBN: 978-1-942896-40-1

PRINT ISBN: 978-1-942896-41-8

Copyright © 2013 Grayton Press

All rights reserved.

Copyeditor: Erica Ellis – inkdeepediting.com

The Pride Series

Finding Pride

Discovering Pride

Returning Pride

Lasting Pride

Serving Pride

Red Hot Christmas

My Sweet Valentine

Return To Me

Rescue Me

The Secret Series

Secret Seduction

Secret Pleasure

Secret Guardian

Secret Passions

Secret Identity

Secret Sauce

The West Series

Loving Lauren

Taming Alex

Holding Haley

Missy's Moment

Breaking Travis

Roping Ryan

Wild Bride

Corey's Catch

Tessa's Turn

The Grayton Series

Last Resort

Someday Beach

Rip Current

In Too Deep

Swept Away

High Tide

Lucky Series

Unlucky In Love

Sweet Resolve

Best of Luck

A Little Luck

Silver Cove Series

Silver Lining

French Kiss

Happy Accident

Hidden Charm

A Silver Cove Christmas

Entangled Series – Paranormal Romance

The Awakening

The Beckoning

The Ascension

Haven, Montana Series

Closer to You

Never Let Go

Holding On

Pride Oregon Series

A Dash of Love

My Kind of Love

Season of Love

Tis the Season

Dare to Love

Where I Belong

Wildflowers Series

Summer Nights

Summer Heat

Stand Alone Books

Twisted Rock

For a complete list of books:

http://JillSanders.com

Jill Sanders is a New York Times, USA Today, and international bestselling author of Sweet Contemporary Romance, Romantic Suspense, Western Romance, and Paranormal Romance novels. With over 55 books in eleven series, translations into several different languages, and audiobooks there's plenty to choose from. Look for Jill's bestselling stories wherever romance books are sold or visit her at jillsanders.com

Jill comes from a large family with six siblings, including an identical twin. She was raised in the Pacific Northwest and later relocated to Colorado for college and a successful IT career before discovering her talent for writing sweet and sexy page-turners. After Colorado, she decided to move south, living in Texas and now making her home along the Emerald Coast of Florida. You will find that the settings of several of her series are inspired by her time spent living in these areas. She has two sons and offset the testosterone in her house by adopting three furry little ladies that provide her company while she's locked in her writing cave. She enjoys heading to the beach, hiking, swimming, wine-tasting, and pickleball with her husband, and of course writing. If you have read any of her books, you may also notice that there is a love of food, especially sweets! She has been blamed for a few added pounds by her assistant, editor, and fans... donuts or pie anyone?

facebook.com/JillSandersBooks

twitter.com/JillMSanders

bookbub.com/authors/jill-sanders